Cook City Publishing Presents:

Queen Bee

By The O.G. Wise Man
&
Keith Young

QUEEN BEE

Urban Literature's New Dynasty

Cook City Publishing

BY THE O.G. WISEMAN

Cook City PublishingCook City Publishing

Urban Literature's New Dynasty

This book is a novel,
Published by

Cook City Publishing, Inc.

545 8th Avenue suite #401
New York, NY 10018-4307
phone # 212-501-2121
Email: cookcity@optonline.net
Copyright 2005

Cook City Publishing

All rights reserved.

Library of Congress
Cataloging-in-Publication Data #2006930499

"Queen Bee"

Summary: TccBee epic; a novel which details the hard knock life of a woman who vows to survive by any means necessary, after the tragic death of her husband she picks up the pieces, reloads her gunz and takes her hustling game to another level. Ride with Darlene!

Paperback
ISBN: 0-9774137-0-5
[1. Crime — Fiction 2. Drama — Fiction 3. Suspense — Fiction]

QUEEN BEE

Editor: **Alese Jackson**
and
Shetalia Miller

Text Formatting:
Shetalia Miller

Cover Design/Graphics:
Brad Agard

Publisher:
Cook City Publishing

First Trade Paperback Edition Printing Aug, 2006

Cook City Publishing

BY THE O.G. WISEMAN

⅄ Word From O.G. Wise Man:

Cook City Publishing

This book is written and dedicated

to all of the women out there

who have kept it gangsta,

on all levels.

If you can feel the struggle,

then ease the pain!

Life goes on,

but real love lasts forever.

Loyalty goes a long way.

Dedications:

This piece of work is dedicated to my mother "The Queen Bee" Dorothy Radcliff. Also Theresa Young. Special recognition goes out to: First and foremost "God" for all of his strength and guidance...without him none of this would be possible. My children Andre D. Moore and Kevae U. Dolphin. My two grandchildren, my two sisters, all of my nephews and nieces, and my great nephews and nieces. Tiffany Young...Bro Darryl "Smash" Ford, Bro Herb. Derrick Young (Flatbush), Anthony "Duke" Burnette, The Uptown Bang Gang, My lil' homie Ross from the motherland. My homeboy Dante. My circle of counselors, Mr. and Mrs. John Mayrant, Aunt "Toot", and my big homeboy Scott "Love" Anderson.

Cook City Publishing

BY THE O.G. WISEMAN

Special shout out goes to those who left me in the belly of the beast when I needed them most! I would like to thank Jay-Z for being a voice inside of my head. Shout out to P. Diddy, Russel Simmons, Baby from Cash Money, and 50 cent for changing the game. One day, we will all be sitting at the same table breaking bread. Shout out to all of the haters... Keep Hating! A distinguished shout out goes to C.C.G. (Cook City Gangstas)! Last but not least, all of the men and women who are in prison! Keep your heed up, strive to make something good of yourself, and always remember that when it seems as if everybody has left you and no one cares, "God" loves you and he is always with you...

Eternally!

QUEEN BEE

FOREWORD

AFTER her husband is violently murdered by the police, Darlene Dennison picks up the pieces, loads her guns, and takes her hustling game to another level.

In this story of money and murder, grind with Darlene as she shakes up the streets of 'Cook City' and makes them her own personal beehive.

The late 70's and early 80's weren't ready for the type of game she put down, but when the games began, anything was liable to happen. When she was on top, everybody danced. No matter what, the hustle must go on!

With a past full of secrets, and a life filled with actors, the strip became one big stage. Darlene vowed to survive; by any means necessary. If you were her friend, then she loved you forever, but woe to the ones that crossed her!

When betrayal sets in, only 'God' could determine the outcome. With the police on her trail, and a District Attorney out to get her, they notoriously named her the 'Queen Bee'.

As this shocking fictional tale takes unpredictable twists and turns, what will be Darlene's fate? In the end, will the streets sing another sad song?

If it's sweetness that you're looking for, then taste this honey. Every page is filled with non-stop suspense.

Cook City Publishing

BY THE O.G. WISEMAN

The life of a woman has never been this hard-lived. When it comes to gangsta bitches, Darlene is at the top of the list.

If you've never been to 'Cook City', then allow the 'Queen Bee' to take you there. But, on your journey, always keep at the forefront of your mind how high the chances are that you might get stung!

Cook City Publishing

QUEEN BEE

CHAPTER ONE

THE BEGINNING

THE RAIN was coming down hard, and Phillip could hardly see through his windshield. Turning the corner at Jefferson and Seneca Streets, he saw the police there, waiting for him. They waved him over. As the two officers approached his car, he slid open the window of his gold 1977 Fleetwood Cadillac.

"What's the reason for this here, officer?" He asked letting his puzzlement show on his face. The cop with the grimacing face immediately took charge. "We had an anonymous tip that you were going to be transporting a large amount of heroin across town, so we would like to search your vehicle."

Phillip didn't sell heroin, and he knew they knew that! The police had been out to get him for a while; the police could not find anything on him, so now they were trying to set him up. He also knew that if they planted some heroin in his car, he would be facing a long term in prison. He thought of the pistol in the inside pocket of his leather coat, knowing eventually, he would use it.

"Would you please step out of the vehicle," the other officer said. As Phillip began to open up the car door to get out, a flash of lightning lit up the sky. The two officers were startled by the sudden clap of thunder, he made his move. Phillip pulled his gun from his jacket, threw the door open, and darted from the car. He heard the shots ring out as the police officers fired at him. He ran down the street, and cut into an alley. The rain was coming down even harder now, and he could hear their splashing footsteps as they pursued him. The officers stopped at the end of the alley, one yelled out, "You might as well give up, we're gonna get your black ass anyway!"

Shots rang out in unison with the thunder claps, Phillip let off five shots in response. Sparks from his .38 special lit up the dark alley and reflected from the damp pavement.

BANG! BANG! PAP! PAP! PAP!

Their shots echoed in the alley. One of the officers hit the ground and rolled through a big puddle of mud. He disappeared into the shadows at the side of the alley. Phillip took his final shot BANG! He started reloading his gun. He never got to finish. The scowling officer had crawled up behind Phillip and shot him in the back of the head; he rose and moved to stand over the body.

QUEEN BEE

The bullet had gone straight through, shattering the skull and taking pieces with it. Falling forward Phillip landed on a row of garbage cans. His pistol was still in his hand; his velour hat rested in a heap of trash. The other officer joined the grimacing one. They quickly investigated the body, and then left the murder scene.

*   *   *

Phillip's car was still in the same place the next morning. A little boy on his way to school found his corpse as the sun was rising. When the police arrived they identified the body, connected him to the car, and then called his wife.

Darlene arrived at the scene just as they were putting Phillip's body into the back of the coroner's van. She looked at the body for a brief moment before she sat down on the curb and cried. Stone-faced, one of the investigating officers approached her. "Are you his wife?"

"Yes," she managed, "Dee—Darlene Dennison"

"As soon as we are finished with the investigation, you can come and pick up the car, ma'am. Two officers will be stopping by your residence later to ask you a couple of questions."

*   *   *

Cook City Publishing

BY THE O.G. WISEMAN

Darlene drove her maroon and white Lincoln Continental home in a daze. Her head spun; she felt like she was drowning in an ocean, "This can't be happening." she said to herself, "How am I going to tell Junior his father is gone? Suddenly she couldn't breathe; gasping for air she turned on the air conditioner. When she arrived at the house, she opened the front door and fell inside. Closing the door with her foot, she lay on the floor and cried until she fell asleep.

Hours later she woke to a knock at the front door. She glanced at her watch it was 2:00p.m., she quickly got herself together and opened the door. Two police officers stood on the other side, she let them in.

"Good afternoon Mrs. Dennison," one of the officers began.
"What's so good about it," she snapped "my damn husband's dead!"
The officer with what seemed a perpetual scowl on his face began the line of irrelevant questions. "Did your husband have any other women on the side Mrs. Dennison?" he asked in a sarcastic tone.
"What? No he didn't, and what does that have to do with what's going on?"
"We just need to know these types of things, they may lead to something. Your husband could have been having an affair with another man's wife, a man who may not have liked that very much."

13

After about two and a half hours of frivolous questions they were finally ready to leave. On their way out the door, the officer with the grimace on his face turned to Darlene, "If there's anything that I can do for you, just give me a call." He handed her his card. Stressed out and aggravated, she threw the card on the floor.

"Just leave!" she screamed, "I won't be needin' you for shit!"
The officer's jaw tightened as he clenched his teeth and squinted, he turned and left.

Half an hour later, Junior came home from school, Dee didn't know how she was going to tell him about his father, but she knew she had to tell him. When he came into the house, she just looked at him and broke down crying. Junior Dennison was the spitting image of his father; he was tall for a 10 year old, he had light brown skin, gray eyes, and a movie star smile. The first thing that came to Darlene's mind when she saw him was, Phillip. She lost all of the words she'd thought to say. After about 15 minutes, she calmed down and pulled herself back together. No longer tongue-tied, she began explaining everything to him, as best she could. With hurt, pain and confusion painted all over his face, Junior asked, "Why did someone kill my dad?"

"I don't know the full story baby, but hopefully, one day we will know the answer to that question."
Junior Dennison was young but he understood

Cook City Publishing

Cook City Publishing

everything that his mother had said. When they were done talking, he went up to his room, cried a little, and prayed to God to give his mother the strength to deal with the situation.

Six days later, Phillip Dennison's funeral took place at Cook City Baptist Church on Fifth and Pfeiffer Streets. All of his family came up from down south to attend the service; he was loved very much by all. Wherever he went, he left his mark, every hustla and gangsta in Cook City was there. Even the pimps and hoes came through to pay their last respects. When the service was over, they all paid their condolences to Darlene, if they didn't give her an envelope filled with money, they kissed her hand and let their respect for her be known. At the burial site, as Phillip's body was being lowered into the ground, Darlene stood there with tears in her eyes. Long after everybody else had left, she fell to her knees and prayed. Memories of her and Phillip flooded her mind...

1963

Phillip Dennison drove his canary yellow Cadillac to Cook City, Pennsylvania from Miami, he looked like a young Denzel Washington.

He stood 6'1, weighed 187 pounds, and wore his jet black hair permed-out and laid to the side under one of his trademark velour hats. No matter what he was dressed in, he always had one to match. When he smiled, the 18-karat gold crown on his bottom front tooth sparkled and glistened. Immediately, he began to lay his game down. Phillip was out to get money and that's all he wanted, he was a hustla in every sense. When he hit 95-North, on his way to Pennsylvania, he had a trunk full of the best weed that came out of Miami. He knew how to get paid, and the 'sticky green' was his main source. Damn near every pimp, hoe, hustla and gangsta loved to smoke reefer, and he had just what they wanted. The first time that he hit the strip, the girls went wild. He was the new face in town, and the aura that he gave off was pure playa. When he cruised down the Sixth Street Strip in his Fleetwood, listening to James Brown, everybody stopped to pay attention. If people didn't already know who he was, they wanted to know. All of the hoes thought he was a pimp, and most of them wanted to be part of his stable.

      A couple of months after straight hustling and blowing the streets of Cook City up with the 'sticky green', Phillip decided to go out and have some fun...

Lingo's Bar on Seventh and Maclay Street was where everybody was hanging out. On Saturday nights they kept one of the liveliest bands up in the joint. Dressed down in an orange three-piece suit, black velour hat and black quarter-cut patent leather boots, he made his debut. That night the strip was jampacked. Cars were illegally parked and the whole nine almost every hoe in the city was patrolling the block, offering her wears. The

Cook City Publishing

pimps were politickin' and the hustlas were doing what they do best. Boppin', through the front door of the bar, the first kat to greet Phillip was Snake Henderson.

"What's goin' on Daddy-O?" the short bowlegged pimp chimed, as he shook Phillip's hand. "I know you got that good reefer for me."

"You know I do," Phillip replied, as he went into the inside pocket of his suit jacket and pulled out a fluffy 'nickel bag'. "Watch how you smoke that shit baby, it'll knock you off ya' feet." They both laughed. After handling his business with Snake, Phillip made his way over to a table near the stage so that he could get a good look at the girl singers in the band. Reaching his desired destination, a fine young, high-yellow broad looked up at him with a pair of the sexiest bedroom eyes he had ever seen.

"You mind if I sit here wit' you baby doll," he asked, while shooting her one of his 'Boss Playa', hypnotizing eye-to-eye contact looks.

"You might as well, before one of these drunk fools up in here try to push up on me, and I definitely ain't havin' that."

Sitting down beside her, Phillip couldn't believe how sexy this young chick was. She can't be old enough to be up in this joint, he thought to himself. Although by looking at her, he could tell why the owner let her in, she was the finest thing in the place. She was about 5'7, with a long blonde wig on. Every time she smiled, her dimples made you wanna pinch her cheeks; her eyes were slightly slanted and looked like pools of still water. The tan mini-skirt she had on was short and so tight that you could see her panty-lines her legs were thicker than tree trunks. The white knee-high stocking's that she wore held everything in place, the brown leather jacket and matching high-heeled boots that she sported complimented her look to the fullest degree.

"What's your name slim?"

"Darlene Sugar, what's yours?"

"My name is Phillip," he answered while lighting up a cigarette. "Can I get you something to drink?"

"Sure, why not. You can get me a cold glass of ripple on the rocks."

After ordering their drinks, they sat and talked for a minute. When the band began playing one of Sam Cook's slow jams, Phillip leaned over and whispered in Darlene's ear, "How about a dance baby?"

"I would love to, sugar." she responded. Out on the dance floor he held her in his arms in the gentlest way. Slowly swaying to the rhythm of the music, they drifted off into their own little world. Just as the song was going into its breakdown, Phillip dipped Darlene and whispered, "I know you wanna be wit' me as bad as I wanna be wit' you. All you have to do is say so."

Darlene became weak in the knees, "Take me, I'm yours baby," she answered as she looked deep into his eyes.

That night, Philip made love to Dee in a way that she

Cook City Publishing

would never forget. From that time forth, they would always be together. He would give her more than any woman could ever ask for, and take her places that she had only imagined she would ever go. Phillip bought her everything from pearl necklaces, to fur coats; he even bought her a brand new Cadillac. Whenever he made his trips to Miami, he would always take her. He allowed Darlene to see everything he was doing, but he would never let her get involved.

In 1967, they had a son. Darlene named him Phillip Dennison, Jr., after his father. Later that same year they got married and Phillip was all that he said he would be. He may have been from 'Down South', but he loved it up in Cook City, he was 25 years old and Darlene was 23; they were building a foundation and Phillip always made sure that it was solid.

In 1971, Phillip opened up a Speakeasy in the basement of their three-story house. It was the most happening spot around. The joint had crap tables, card tables, a jukebox, a bar, a pinball machine, and the whole nine. He even built a secret exit into the wall, so that if the cops ever raided the place, there would always be an escape route.
Darlene had heard a lot of stories about Phillip and what he did to people that owed him money, but she never witnessed any of it until one day down in the speakeasy...

QUEEN BEE

With a full-blown crap game in progress, a nigga named Roy snatched up all the bets off the table after he crapped out.

"Roy, what the fuck is you doin'?!" Phillip shouted, "If you don't put that muthafuckin' money back down on that table, I'm gonna cut you a new asshole!"

"Man, fuck you and the rest of these lames!" Roy shouted back, gripping the bundle of money up tight in his hand.

Phillip hit his back pocket twice, WOP! WOP!, and came out with his switchblade, with two vicious strikes, he came across Roy's neck. Blood spurted everywhere.

"Nigga didn't I tell you to put that money back down?"

Roy fell to his knees with a pitiful look in his eyes, begging and pleading, "Please Phillip man, I'm sorry baby, please don't kill me...pleeease!"

After Roy dropped the money back down on the table, he looked up at Phillip through teary eyes.

"Get yo' muthafuckin' ass outta my spot, and don't come back around here no more!"

Scrambling to his feet Roy ran up the steps, out of the basement and down the street, seeing the incident, Darlene knew that Phillip wasn't to be fucked with, in no kind of way.

For years, the Speakeasy ran smoothly without any interference from the police. Then, one day, they just

Cook City Publishing

showed up. As the cops stormed through the front door, Phillip quietly got everybody out through the secret passage in the basement. They never arrested anybody but him, and they never found anything but beer and liquor.

The police wanted Phillip out of the way, they would harass him anywhere they saw him especially when he was with Darlene. They would always try to embarrass him in front of her, so that he would react and give them some real cause to dispose of him. One cop really had it out for him; this cop would always go out of his way to mess with Phillip. The officer would scratch-up Phillip's car, bust the headlights out and write him traffic tickets at every opportunity. Darlene didn't like what was going on between Phillip and the police; she always felt that something bad was going to happen.

In the spring of 1977, that something did happen and after Phillip's tragic death, Darlene's life would never be the same.

*   *   *

AFTER DARLENE returned home from Phillip's burial site, her two sisters Danielle and Dameka were waiting for her at the house with Junior. When she came in, she hugged Junior, and went upstairs to lay down. While she was laying down in the bed she kept looking at the poster-sized picture of her and Phillip down in Miami, crying hysterically, she didn't know what she was going to do, she had a lot of mixed emotions. Phillip was her world and now he was gone. One minute she was sad, the next she was mad she got out of the bed and began to pace the floor. She couldn't prove it, but she was willing to bet her life that the police had something to do with killing Phillip. Not to mention, she knew that he would never allow anyone to get close enough to do something like that.

After she laid back down for a while, Darlene drifted off to sleep. When she woke up it was almost midnight, her mind was racing and she picked up right where she had left off.

Her first worries were of Junior "How am I going to raise him by myself? What will become of us? Phillip had left some money, but how long would that last?" Darlene felt herself getting angry again she held her head in her hands. Thinking about the whole situation, and how Phillip would want her to handle it, she made a vow to survive. "I will do whatever it takes, me and my son will never want for anything."

Darlene thought about how Phillip ran his game, and knew that she had to keep the hustle running. Contemplating for a while she got up out of her bed, went over to the dresser, and picked up Phillip's black book. The phone number for his weed connection was in there, and she would use it when the time was right. Phillip still had about 80 pounds of reefer in the stash

Cook City Publishing

that would hold her down for a good minute. For the rest of the night, she sat up putting her plan together on how she was going to put her game down. She had two younger sisters and she knew that they would give her all of the help she needed. She was a woman and she knew it would be hard for her to put her game down the way Phillip had. She would have to keep the streets of Cook City supplied with weed, and also be able to keep the speakeasy running. She knew that it would take all that she had and she was willing to give her life.

The next morning when Danielle, Dameka and Junior woke up, Darlene said, "Don't nobody say nothing until I'm done. Ya'll already know that Phillip was gettin' his hustle on. Y'all also know about the speakeasy that we got down stairs in the basement, Phillip is gone and it's my game now. I gotta do what must be done to take care of my son and I need both of y'all to be down all the way. Danielle I will need you to help me run the Speakeasy. I will show you everything that has to be done; you will also learn how to run the crap table too. Dameka, I will need your help runnin' the weed spot. It's a non-stop thing but I know you can handle it, after you get used to it, you will be able run it with ease. Y'all are all I got, and I need y'all to have my back. It might get rough at times, but it can't get rougher than us. If it ever comes to gunplay, Phillip left me plenty of pistols; I want y'all to always keep it real with the people that we deal with. But if anybody ever crosses us, that's their ass! I want people to love us more than they hate us, if they love us they will always be down for us, if they hate us then we will have to watch our backs and together we will be able to lock these streets down. Can y'all feel me or what?"

"Sis, you know we got your back." Dameka added, "If this is the game that we gotta play then we gonna play it to the fullest."

James, Darlene, Danielle and Dameka were born to Ralph and Georgia Sawyers of Winston-Salem, North Carolina. James was the oldest of the four siblings, then there was Darlene, Danielle was next and Dameka was the youngest. At the age of 16, James Sawyers was gunned down in cold blood in front of his younger sister Danielle, who often accompanied him to places their mother and father forbid them to go. Virginia's Juke Joint, deep in the backwoods was where the brutal killing had taken place. The disastrous incident changed the whole structure of their family; it left them without a younger male role model for the girls to look up to. Without her older brother around, 15-year old Darlene had to take on the responsibility of most of the chores as well as looking after her two younger sisters. After Going to school every morning, helping Danielle and Dameka with their schooling, and then going to work in the cotton fields for Mr. Brooks for the rest of the day, Darlene developed an unyielding characteristic most girls her age didn't have. The money that she earned

Cook City Publishing

from working in the fields went towards the family's upkeep of their tiny farm. The farm sat three miles away from the one room school building that Darlene and her two sisters went to each day. After observing the way their daughter Darlene handled the situation, Mr. and Mrs. Sawyers knew that she would grow up with the ability to obtain all of the things that she wanted from life.

More than anyone else in the family, Danielle had definitely been affected, witnessing the murder of her brother, out of everyone she felt the closest to him. In fact, she considered him her hero. Danielle saw James do things that she imagined no one else in the world could do. Even though she was just a little girl, she adopted most of his ways. When no one was around she would often imitate some of the things she had seen him do. Watching how masterfully James shot dice, Danielle picked up the game very quickly often simulating the two square bones with rocks. In various ways her big brother shaped and molded her outlook on life, helping her to develop the traits that would become a major part of her make-up.

10-year old Dameka was devastated by the tragedy of her brother's death; she loved her brother in so many ways, and for so many reasons. Without him being around, there was a gap in her life that could only be replaced by a similar type of warmth and giving. Even though she still had the rest of the family for support, none of them were able to instill the confidence that

Cook City Publishing

*he had given her. It was extremely difficult for Darlene,
Danielle and Dameka to survive without their brother
there to guide and protect them in the very racially
segregated southern town they lived in. Nevertheless,
Darlene sucked it up and helped her mother and father
raise her two younger sisters as best as she could,
always remembering a lot of the things that her brother
had taught her. At times the cold winters became
unbearable, the harvest time in the spring produced
barely enough for them to survive on. Being both God-
fearing people, Ralph and Georgia Sawyers believed
that 'He' would provide for and take care of them all.
However, each day it seemed as if things for the family
only got worse. Just after her 16th birthday, Darlene
decided that she would help her mother and father out
tremendously. Doing all that she could, she managed
to save some money from different odd jobs that she
had been hired to do in the city. A lot of them were
deplorable and degrading, but never once did she falter.
Darlene took her two sisters and moved them 'up North'
to a place that she had often heard her brother James
talk about. Mr. and Mrs. Sawyers didn't want their
children to go, but they knew within their hearts that it
would be the best thing for their daughters to do.
Arriving in Cook City, Pennsylvania, Darlene quickly
found employment scrubbing floors and doing
laundry for the pregnant housewives of the prominent
businessmen who lived in the downtown area. She also
found a one room sufficient enough for her and her two*

Cook City Publishing

BY THE O.G. WISEMAN

sisters to live in. After a few months of this she landed a full-time job as a nighttime cleaning woman at Beck's Department Store and was able to move them into a small two bedroom apartment right off of Fifth and Reilly Streets. Having Danielle and Dameka enrolled in school, she made sure they always learned as much as they could. If she couldn't give them her all, then she wouldn't give them anything at all. Along the way, Darlene had her share of bad relationships with no good men who were only out to get what they could from her. The South had been so cold and miserable, and in many ways she was glad that she had taken her chances by migrating to Cook City. After a few more-than-forgettable relationships in the mid 1960's, Darlene met the man of her dreams. She allowed 16-year old Danielle and 14-year old Dameka take over the apartment and decided to pursue her longing desire for true happiness.

NOW, ALMOST 12 YEARS LATER, and after the death of Phillip they were back together again. Danielle was 28 years old, dark brown-skinned, about 5'8, with hazel eyes. Her body was tight, and she was much more tits than ass. Dameka was just a touch lighter, 5'6 with a body like a young country girl. She was so thick that she had to get her mini-skirts specially made. The average kat running around in the streets didn't have a chance of getting next to them, and they knew it. Fate had again placed the three sisters at a crossroad, but life

Cook City Publishing

27

had greatly improved for them since their tearful exodus from the hardscrabble backwoods of North Carolina and its overt ménage of blatant racism and ever-long misery. The tragedy of Phillip's murder threatened to bring their new, hard-found life crashing savagely to the ground. Same as it was then, it was Darlene who was navigating their way through the darkness of uncertainty. After she had shared her vision for their survival, the discussions were over, Danielle and Dameka hugged Darlene tightly and kissed her on each cheek, almost as loving daughters would a much-adored mother.

Cook City Publishing

BY THE O.G. WISEMAN

Cook City Publishing

CHAPTER TWO

THE MONEY

THE FOLLOWING day, it was time to get the money. Coming back from the stash spot where Phillip stored his weed, Dee picked Danielle and Dameka up at the house. She took both of them down to the weed spot, and showed them how it was supposed to be run. The spot was a two-story, red brick house, with black metal bars on the window and the screen door. It was located on 3rd Street, between Kelker and Hamilton Streets. The only furnishings were a floor-model television, a couch, a chair, a loveseat and a coffee table in the front room.

The dining room and upstairs bedrooms were empty. The only other room that contained appliances was the kitchen. It had a table, three chairs, a refrigerator and a microwave oven.

"Dameka, go back outside and get that green duffel bag out of the trunk," Darlene said as she walked around the spot, inspecting the place. After opening the trunk, and picking up the duffel bag, Dameka fumbled.

"Girl, this damn thing is heavy as a muthafucka! What you got in here, bricks?" she laughed.

"Ain't no tellin'," Danielle said, as she rushed to the front door to help her sister. When Danielle and Dameka got back inside the house with the bag, Darlene turned on the kitchen light and pulled out the three chairs.

"Sit the bag down on the floor next to the table," she said to Dameka, while heading towards the refrigerator. After grabbing the container of Sunny D-light orange juice and some glasses out of the cabinet above the stove, she returned to the table and quickly unzipped the bag.

"Damn!" Danielle exclaimed as she looked at the 20 pounds of weed that occupied the bag. With a look of pure bewilderment, Dameka moved closer, "that's a lot of muthafuckin' weed, girl!"

Not wasting any time on small talk, Dee began placing pound after pound of refer on the table.

"Danielle, get that scale out from up under the sink, and grab the sandwich bags out of the top drawer. We gotta break most of this shit down and get it ready to be sold."

She showed Dameka how to bag up 'nickels', 'dimes' and 'twenties', while she and Danielle bagged up 'quarters', 'halves', and whole ounces. They also bagged up a couple of 'quarter and a half' pounds. Three and a half hours later, they were done, and Darlene opened up shop. She opened up the front door, but kept the screen locked. Whenever somebody came to the spot to buy weed, they would drop their money through the small metal slot in the screen door, and the product would get slid back to them. The only time that anyone was allowed inside the spot was if they were buying a quarter of a pound or more. When the front door was closed, that meant there was nothing happening. But when it was open, it was on and poppin'!

The spot hadn't been open more than five minutes when the money started flowing.

"What's happening' Dee?" Freddy said as he dropped $20 through the metal slot of the screen door.

"The money. Nothin', but the money," she responded, as she slid a fat sack of 'sticky green' out to him.

Immediately, the traffic began to flow in $5, $10, $20, $80, $40, $10, $200, $40, $5, $20, $800, $10, $5, and on and on the money kept coming. When things finally did slow down, they closed the front door, locked up shop and went back up to the Speakeasy.

Standing behind the bar, Darlene looked over at Danielle and said "This should be a little easier for you to do than what Dameka has to do. The only time that it gets a little hectic is when gamblers come through. Most of the time I will be here to help you and when I'm not, you will just have to hold it down."

She showed Danielle where all of the liquor and beer

was and how much everything cost, from a shot of wine, to a half-pint. She showed her everything from A-to-Z, and then she showed her how to run the crap table. Danielle already knew how to shoot dice, so she caught on to the house game very quickly. The last thing Dee showed her two younger sisters was the secret exit that Phillip had built into the wall. When she removed the panel and slid the wall to the side, Dameka was astonished.

"Damn, that nigga Phillip was on top of his game," she said, as she walked back and forth through the passage.

"Yeah, he definitely was. Now we gotta be on top of ours, my baby paved the way for the shit we are gettin' ready to put into effect."
After showing her sisters how to open and close the exit, Darlene sat them down one more time.

"What we are getting ready to do has never been done before. This is some serious business, and we must always keep that in mind. Now that everything has been put into proper perspective, the game has begun."
Danielle stood up "Well, let's play baby girl, let's play!"
Dameka leaned back in her chair and winked her right eye, "Lets get that muthafuckin' money!"

While all of this was going on, Junior Dennison had his hands full at school. He had gotten into a real nasty scuffle with a kid named Jerry from 4th Street. Jerry was young, wild and stocky; he was known for bullying other kids. When he tried to take some of Junior's candy, Junior punched him right in the eye.

"Man, yo' punk ass ain't taking' nothin' from me," Junior said as he threw up his hands to defend himself. Shaking off the effects of the first blow and clearing his vision, Jerry shouted as he spat on the ground, "Now I'm gonna take all your shit, bitch!"
Throwing a wild punch, Junior slipped and grabbed his left pant leg. When he yanked, Jerry fell flat on his back. Junior dashed on top of him.

"I told yo' punk ass that you ain't gettin' nothin' from me!" he yelled as he punched Jerry in the sides and the back of his head.
Crowds of kids were now starting to gather around. Most of them were happy to see Junior stand up to the schoolyard bully. After a little bit of twisting and squirming, Jerry was able to make it back to his feet. Swaying staggering from side to side, he had knots and lumps all over his head. Feeling really confident now, Junior said "After I finish with you, ain't nobody gonna be scared of you."
Jerry lazily threw another punch at him, but this time Junior blocked it and hit him with an overhand right. Jerry went down. All of the young kids were screaming and cheering. Before Junior could jump on him again, the bus pulled up and Jerry ran and hopped on it. Junior looked down at his clothes, 'Damn! My mom's gonna kill me when she sees this,' he thought to himself. He knew that she was gonna to be mad, but he also knew

that she wouldn't be mad for too long. His father had taught him to never let anyone hurt him, and he never would.

Later on that night, Dameka had the weed spot pumpin'. People were still coming through just like they were when Darlene first opened up shop. Before Darlene dropped her off at the spot, she gave Dameka a .38 special chrome revolver.

"This is your best friend girl; always keep it by your side. If something don't seem right, let that muthafucka' smoke!"

"Don't worry about me sis, if I have any problems, I'ma put a cap in somethin'."

At about 1:30am, when Dameka was about to close up shop, this slick, slim-ass nigga came up to the door and dropped $80 through the slot.

"What's shaking' lil' momma, I ain't never seen you before." he crooned with a West Coast accent. "Is Dee yo' people or something?"

"Who's asking," she probed while sliding him the ounce of weed through the slot.

"My name is George Pharrel, but you can call me Pharrel."

Dameka's nipples stood hard and erect as she looked at him, "Where you from Pharrel?"

"I'm from L.A. baby; I've been out this way for about a year. That nigga Phillip was my man, we made plenty of down low moves together."

Dameka damn near handed him her pussy on a platter

after she heard that. A couple of minutes later, she opened the door and let him in. All the while thinking, as she looked him up and down, *'I got plans for this nigga, but first I'ma give him a slice of this brown sugar pussy.'* She could tell Pharrel was a hustla by the way he swaggered. If he's a true hustla, then I'ma have him hustlin' for me, she thought to herself. For the next 45 minutes or so, they sat and talked. Then Dameka got up and closed the front door. Calling Darlene on the phone, she informed her that everything was cool and that she would be home late, just as soon as she took care of some business.

Walking back into the front room she stopped and gave Pharrel a tongue-tasty look, "If I gave you some of this pussy, you wouldn't know what to do with it," she teased.

Leaning back on the couch, crossing his legs like a pimp, Pharrel replied, "If you gave me some of that pussy; you wouldn't know what to do."

Immediately, Dameka walked over to the end table and turned off the lamp. The only light left in the room was from the television and as she slid out of her black miniskirt, Pharrel adored her soft, smooth, thick, irresistible hips.

"Damn, lil' momma, you sho' nuff got somethin' there," he said anxiously as he felt his nature rise.

Completely naked, Pharrel couldn't believe his eyes, "You think you can handle this wild kitten, playa?" she purred, rubbing her hand between her legs, massaging her moistening, velvety treasure chest.

"If I can't, I'm damn sure gonna try!"
In that instant, the fuck-fest began. Dameka threw that cabbage patch on Pharrel; back to back she had that nigga cummin'. He released three times before she let off once; when he got soft she got him hard again. Pharrel may have been a playa from out of L.A., but he wasn't ready for the type of sex game that Dameka was playing. The kitten was too wild for him to tame. "AAAAAAHHHH!" She released herself, and they started all over again. Three hours later, Pharrel dropped Dameka off at the house. She kissed him softly on the lips and told him to call her the next day. When she got inside the house, she excitedly told Darlene and Danielle the whole story.

"Girl, y'all should have seen the way I threw this thang on that nigga! He didn't know if he was cummin' or goin'!" They laughed.
When they were done talking, they all headed upstairs, and went to bed.

Thursday night, Darlene came up with a brilliant idea; Phillip had been on her mind constantly for the last couple of days. As they were closing up the Speakeasy, she looked up from counting the day's profit and said, "We gonna have the liveliest muthafuckin' party this town has ever had. We gonna make sure that they always remember Phillip. Y'all let everybody know that it's goin' down!"

BY THE O.G. WISEMAN

Cook City Publishing

*   *   *

Saturday night, the speakeasy was overflowing with hustlas, playas, ballas and pimps. The sisters had expected the party to be big, but they never imagined such a turnout.
The jukebox had everybody steppin' to the same smooth groove. Through a hazy cloud of weed smoke, Darlene and her sisters made their entrance down the basement steps, dressed to kill. Darlene led the way in a gold and red checkered mini-skirt and a clingy backless gold turtleneck top. Her head was chicly swathed in an elegant turban of gold. Her gold knee-high stiletto go-go boots looked as if they had just been freshly minted; setting the ensemble ablaze was the ruby and diamond necklace, earrings and bracelet that Phillip had bought her for her 21st birthday. Danielle had on a one-piece black and white skirt set with a cut out back. In 6" high heeled white leather ankle boots and knee-high stockings, she was the reincarnation of Cleopatra Jones. Dameka was visibly nude under her red skin-tight suede cat suit. Her ass was so fat, that when she walked, it seemed like it was calling you. The red leather boots, with gleaming gemstone side buckles made her look like she just stepped off a stage. The auburn wig added to her excruciatingly exotic beauty. The message was unmistakable, Darlene and her sisters were some bad

ass bitches, and everybody knew it.

When the O'Jays record, 'She Used To Be My Girl', came on, the dance floor got packed. Everybody was bumping and grinding to the highest degree. Dameka shut the dance floor down when she pulled Pharrel out into the crowd and started shaking her thang.

"Work it baby!" Leo the wino yelled from over in the corner where he was sipping on his own personal quart of Thunderbird, boppin' and dippin'. Dameka was doing her own special rendition of the 'The Bump', swaying her thick hips from side to side. Danielle had her hands full with a couple of playas from Tennessee; they both got tired of trying to keep up with her. After the song ended, Darlene turned off the jukebox and asked if she could have everyone's attention.

"To all you playas, hoes, hustlas, gangstas and pimps, I wanna thank y'all for coming out and partying with us. As ya'll already know, this whole she-bang is in dedication to my deceased husband and main man, Phillip. All of ya'll that got drinks in ya'll hands, toast it up to one of the realest hustlas who ever walked the streets of Cook City!"

Everybody drank whatever they had in their hands, and then cheered in one deafening voice, "AIN'T NO PARTY LIKE A COOK CITY PARTY!"

"Ya'll enjoy ya'selves, and have a glass of ripple on Phillip!" Darlene turned the music back on and everybody started dancing again.

Opening the bathroom door, Danielle caught this trick

Cook City Publishing

giving Chico some head.

"Man, what the fuck do ya'll think this is, a hoe house or somethin'?! Let me get in this bitch so I can use the bathroom!"
Looking at Danielle from down on her knees, the young trick quickly got up and hurried back downstairs.

"Chico, you old, no good bastard, you! I'm surprised yo' dick didn't fall off by now," she joked as she squeezed past him and sat down on the toilet.

While Darlene was upstairs sitting down at the kitchen table, gathering her thoughts, Doe slid up on her and tried to spit some weak-ass game at her.   "Nigga, if you don't carry yo' ass up outta here! You ain't got nothin' for me; you ain't even on my level. If you knew how sad yo' ass looked, you would check ya'self!" she laughed. Doe stepped off.
The party lasted until 5:30a.m.; almost everybody was staggering on their way out. Darlene, Dameka and Danielle were at the door. Leo the wino was the last one to leave. Stumbling up to the door, he stopped in front of Darlene.

"Dee, I want you to know that Phillip was the realest kat I ever met. He always showed a no good nigga like me love. When nobody else wanted to be bothered with me, he would always give me couple of dollars so that I could get somethin' to eat."
Pausing for a moment, Leo drifted down memory lane…

QUEEN BEE

"Leo, what the fuck you doin' standing out in the damn rain nigga?" Phillip asked, as he pulled up to the corner of Sixth and Hamilton, rolling down the car window.

"Where the fuck I'm gonna go?" Leo replied. "They just put me out the Grill 'cause I ain't got no money to buy nothin' to eat! My sister told me don't come the fuck around the house until I get myself together."

"You in a fucked up situation, old nigga! Hop the fuck in here wit' me and get outta the rain!"
In disbelief at Phillip's generosity inviting him to get inside the clean Cadillac, Leo hesitated, looking down at his filthy attire and dirty shoes.

"Man, if you don't get the fuck in here! I ain't worried about that bullshit!" Phillip said.
Running to the passenger-side of the car, Leo opened the door and got in with a big-ass 'Kool-Aid' smile on his face. Phillip could smell the wino's foul odor. Nevertheless, he overlooked it and pulled off.

"How long have you been out here in the streets old nigga?" Phillip casually began as Marvin Gaye whispered through the car speakers in the background.

Shit, I'm fifty-one now; I ain't never had nobody care for me! My sister Darla is the only family I know. She damn near sixty years old, and she been cussin' me out for forty-four of them!"

"You been around for a while Leo. I know you seen a lot change in this city!"

"What! Man, I remember when black's wasn't

Cook City Publishing

allowed in this part of town! This section used to be all white! I done been arrested so many times for frivolous shit it ain't funny!"

"You should be about tired then, huh?"

"Tired ain't the word, youngsta'. I'm worn out! But what else is it for an old dog to do! I don't know any new tricks! Phillip, man, you just don't know what I've been through!" Wiping his dirty sleeve across his even more dirty and haggard face, Leo prevented his burning eyes from crying. "This shit ain't been fun at all! When you drink as much wine as I do, you become addicted to it. You see how I be shakin' sometimes when I come down to the speakeasy early in the morning to get my first shot! I need that before I can even think about putting some food in my stomach."

Looking at the gray-headed wino, Phillip thought about some of the tribulations he had faced as a young kid back in Florida, and in some ways he could relate to Leo.

"I can't tell you what to do baby, you damn near lived twice my lifetime! But what I'm gonna say is that you need to get ya'self together. Ya sister ain't gonna be around forever, nigga! After she gone, what you gonna do then?"

Leo sat somberly in the passengers' side of the Cadillac with his head hung low, listening to the sincere and piercing words from this man he barely knew. Spinning back around the block and stopping in front of the Hamilton Grill restaurant, Phillip peeled off $300 and

41

handed it to Leo.

"Go in there and you get something to eat, nigga. And get the fuck out of the rain. If I see you standin' out here when I float back by, I'ma really make it rain down on yo' ass!"

Leo didn't know what to say as he looked down at the wad of dollars that Phillip had just handed him. Knowing that the old man appreciated the kind gesture, but couldn't find the words to show his gratitude, Phillip grinned, "Go ahead man, take yo' ass in the Grill and get somethin' to eat. Stop by the speakeasy and holla at me later on!"

Leo returned from his memory of Phillip teary-eyed and smiling facing the three slightly confused sisters. He had drifted off into his reverie mid-sentence, while bidding the ladies goodnight. Regaining himself, he exhaled deeply, "I was just remembering how that nigga looked out for the old-head once. I will never forget that nigga. Ever! You a good woman and he would want you to have the world. Go get it, girl."

Now openly blubbering, Leo staggered out the door, leaving behind a very touched and proud widow.

*   *   *

MONDAY MORNING, Darlene was on the phone with the weed connect from Florida. After she hung up, she

Cook City Publishing

Cook City Publishing

looked over at her two sisters who were cleaning and reassembling their pistols. "We gotta take a trip. Ya'll be ready to leave tonight."

When Junior came home from school Darlene informed him that he would be staying with his friend Barry for the next couple of nights. At 8:00p.m. that night, they dropped Junior off and hit 95-South.

"The niggas that we dealing with ain't no joke. They straight up and they about they business." Dee said.

"Shit, we about our business too," Dameka said defensively. "If anything goes to the left I'ma light somethin' the fuck up, and make it right!"

Danielle cocked her .44 magnum and added, "I would hate to bring darkness to one of them niggas lives."

Arriving in Miami the next evening, the sisters checked into the four-star Hampton Inn Hotel and unpacked their bags. At 12:00am that same night, Patrick met them down in the main lobby of the hotel. Dameka and Danielle felt the same sexual sensation as they eyed the brown-skinned, dreadlocked Jamaican standing before them with his solid, muscular six-foot frame.

"Good evening ladies, I hope that you had a nice trip. Let's go outside and get into my car." Looking directly at Darlene he continued, "I am sorry about Phillip. I owe him much respect. I will show you how much through my dealings with you."

Taking a back road out into the countryside, twenty-five minutes later they arrived at Patrick's farmhouse. It sat on ten acres of land, and was completely surrounded by a 6'0 red, black and a green picket fence.

After entering the front gate, and pulling up to the entrance, four other Jamaican kats came out of the house to meet them. Dameka and Danielle did not say too much of anything. They were alert and on point at all times. Danielle had her .44 in her purse, cocked and ready to blow. Dameka was packing a black metal German Luger and Darlene had two twin .22 chrome Dillingers with pearl handles. One was tucked away in her bra and the other was concealed on the inside of her right boot. The Jamaicans were Phillip's people, but he was gone now and she didn't trust anybody.

Seating all three of the women at a long wooden conference table in the main office of the house, Patrick went back outside and retrieved a couple of pounds of product.

"Damn, this smells like some good shit," Danielle said after Darlene passed her a pound of the weed to examine.

"This is some good 'sticky green' here. We definitely gonna come up off this," Dameka added as she pulled a few buds from the bag.

"I need two hundred pounds of this shit," Darlene stated. "I know you can handle that."

"If you have forty thousand, then I have the amount you are looking for."

After opening her Anne Klein suitcase and counting $40,000 out of it, Darlene and Patrick made the

Cook City Publishing

Cook City Publishing

transaction. He provided them with their own personal U-Haul truck equipped with furniture concealing the weed.

"You ladies drive carefully. You have a lot of merchandise in this truck. Out of respect for Phillip, I gave you a grand deal."

"Much respect. I will call you when I need you," Darlene smiled.
Early the next morning they were on the highway. Darlene and Dameka were driving the U-Haul truck and Danielle drove the car. The first thing that Darlene did on her return home was to pick Junior up.

"Hey baby," she cooed as he ran into her arms and kissed her. "I can tell that you missed me just as much as I missed you."
She presented him with all of the T-shirts she had bought for him in Miami. All of them had some crazy type of writing on them, Junior really loved his gifts. After talking with his mother for a while and asking her a million questions he went upstairs took a bath and went to bed.
After being closed during the trip to Miami, the speakeasy had a nice crowd when it reopened. The gamblers fell through the spot first and it seemed that everybody else followed. Big Bo, Country and Sandy Clark had a pocket full of money and they were ready to gamble. When Country came down the steps and saw Big Bo and Sandy, it was on.

"What ya' niggas tryin' to do? I got a fat-ass

bankroll and I'm trying' to win some mo'!"

"Nigga, you ain't said nothin'!" Big Bo yelled, "Let the crap game begin!"

"Let me get the muthafuckin' dice Danielle! Somebody gonna leave this bitch broke tonight," Sandy Clark said as he pulled a bankroll of $20, $50 and $100 bills out of his pocket.

"Ya'll niggas just hold up and let me get the crap table set straight. I don't want no muthafuckin' arguin' in this muthafucka either!" Hearing Sandy Clark ramble on triggered a memory in Danielle from when she was a little girl...

"Boy, them damn dice was loaded!" Paul Lee accused, looking at James with hatred in his eyes.

"Ain't no way you made all them damn points in a row like that!"

"Didn't you shoot the dice too?!" James roared back. "You just mad I took yo' last two dollars!" Standing next to the back steps at Virginia's Juke Joint, James was dressed in a pair of secondhand gray knickerbockers, a worn gray shirt, an oversized applejack hat that he had won from Franky Mims the week before and a pair of scuffed up brown buckle up shoes. His green eyes sparkled from the small fire that burned a few feet away from where the garbage was tossed. His unforgettable smile made him look as if he was out of place in the wooded area. He looked as if he belonged in the city somewhere.

Cook City Publishing

46

BY THE O.G. WISEMAN

"You gonna give me my money back, boy!" Paul Lee threatened, approaching James with his fist balled up. *"I know a bad pair of dice when I see 'em!"*

"I beat you fair and square, Paul Lee! I ain't never cheated at no craps!"

Paul Lee knew that James was telling the truth. He also knew that there was nothing wrong with the white pair of dice. However, he just couldn't go back home without his grandmother's groceries, she had sent him out to Emma Mae's to pick up an order that she had placed a couple of weeks ago. Along the way, he had decided to gamble with her money and had lost it. Now, he was faced with a serious problem and was trying to bully his money back from the smaller younger boy.

"I ain't fixin' ta' stand here and keep arguing wit' you James! Now gimme back my two dollars so I can go!" Paul Lee demanded. Sitting a few feet away on a small tree stump, watching the whole scene, 12-year old Danielle knew that the big, black 'peasy' head boy was lying about her brother James cheating at the crap game. One thing that he always stressed to her was never to be known as a cheat at anything she did.

"If you can't win fair and square, then it's just not meant for you to win!"

"Now I done told you, Paul Lee, I ain't cheated you outta nothin' and you ain't gettin' nothin' back from me!" James answered, getting fed up with the bogus accusation.

"So, that's what it's gonna be, huh?!" Just as

James started to say something, Paul Lee unexpectedly threw a wild overhand right at him, catching James on the right side of the head.

Stumbling backwards, James managed to maintain his balance. Striking out at James again, Paul Lee missed with a lazy left jab. Danielle jumped up off the tree stump with an urge to help her brother, but a sharp look from him quickly discouraged her.

Taking his time, James studied Paul Lee before giving two left hooks to the body, and a right across to the head. The tall, dark-skinned boy fell like a freshly cut apple tree.

"Get 'em James!" Danielle shouted before placing her hand over her mouth, hoping she hadn't made her brother mad at her for speaking out of turn. Realizing that he had Paul Lee hurt, James went to finish him off. Just as he went to leap on the older boy, Paul Lee pulled out a taped up, barely useable .22 Derringer and fired, catching James square in the chest. The odd sound of the little gun startled Danielle, as she watched her brother grab his heart and drop to the ground. Looking around to see if anyone had seen what had taken place Paul Lee leaped up, ran over to James, retrieved the money from his pockets and fled through the woods.

"JAMES! JAMES! JAMES! GET UP JAMES!" Danielle screamed, crawling over to her brother's side as he lay on the ground in a pool of blood holding his chest, with his eyes wide open.

Cook City Publishing

48

BY THE O.G. WISEMAN

"JAMES! JAMES! JAAAAAMES!" she shrieked some more and hot tears began to gush as she realized that he wasn't with her anymore.

"Hey! Where you at girl? Can I get my drink now?!"

After serving a couple of people their drinks, Danielle got the crap game started. Country grabbed the dice and bucking everything on them; he even laid Big Bo $500 to $300 odds that he would hit a 10 or 4. While all eyes were focused on the games, this smooth-ass hustla named Corey from Green Street came dippin' down the steps and slid up to the crap table. He pulled out a stack of hundred dollar bills and sat them down in front of him. Dressed down in a money-green double-breasted three piece Armani suit, he vaguely resembled Snoop Dogg. Danielle was running the game, but she couldn't keep her eyes off him. *'Damn, this nigga is fine,'* she thought to herself.

When it was Corey's turn to shoot the dice he grabbed 'em, looked up at Danielle, and blew a kiss. Danielle's mind started working as she sized Corey up. He was kind of tall with a slim build and permed-out hair, although he was in his 30's; he had the face of a young boy.

"We ain't gonna play no games," he said. "Bet everything I got on the table."

"Whatever it is, I'm covering it nigga, shoot the dice!" Country hollered. A minute later, he was walking

Cook City Publishing

up the steps on his way to his stash, to get the rest of the $9,000 that he owed Corey for covering his bet.
When the crap game was over everybody left and when Country got back, Corey and Danielle were the only ones there. Handing Corey the $3,500 he owed, he broke out and now was the time for Danielle to make her move. She walked over to the booth where Corey was seated counting his money, and slid down beside him.

"What was that kiss all about earlier, nigga?" If anybody can fade you, it's me. If you tryin' to see what I'm workin' wit', all you gotta do is ask." Corey paused from counting his money and looked up, "Ain't nobody here but me and you. The dice is over there on the table." Getting up from the booth and grabbing the dice, Danielle shook them hard. "Bet ya stack playa, winner takes all. If you win, I will give you a bonus."

"Bet it." With a soft blow and a slow roll, she let the dice go, bouncing off the wood and landing on seven, she whispered, "door blow, baby." Corey was fucked up. All the money that he had just won, he turned around and lost to a bitch. Picking the stacks up from the table, Danielle smiled, "Even though you lost, I'm gonna give you the bonus anyway cause I like you." She sashayed over to the jukebox and pressed L-7. Isaac Hayes began to play. She began her show. The only thing that she took off was her white silk blouse; she left her red mini-skirt and white boots on. Corey was stuck when he saw how perfectly shaped her breasts

Cook City Publishing

were. Teasingly she said, "Pretty, ain't they?" Slowly rubbing on them in a circular motion she continued, "I don't need yo' money nigga, I got my own paper don't get it fucked up, but you can help me with a few other things."

"If I can lil' momma, I definitely will." Danielle slid out of her skirt and danced for him with nothing but boots on. When the song was over, she sat up on the table in front of him with her legs wide open. "Taste it," she said, as she leaned her head back and closed her eyes. Corey stuck his face in between her legs and began to work his tongue with expertise. After a few moments Danielle stood up, poked her ass out and leaned over the table.

"Let me see what you can do with that." Corey tried, but she was too much for him. Exercising the muscles in her pussy, she brought him to an immediate climax, ten minutes later she was telling him what she needed to be done on the hustling tip.

"I'm always down to get a lil' paper, especially with a fine ass broad like you. I got my spot down on Green Street and we can make plenty of money out of that bitch. I already know who your sisters are, so you know I know what type of money is involved."

"You dealin' wit' me," she stated. "If anything goes wrong, I'ma be the one you see not them you dig. An hour later, she hit Corey off with ten pounds of weed. Now she and her sisters had two soldiers. If everything went right, she knew that it wouldn't take them any time to get rid of their product.

Darlene was impressed with the way her two sisters were handling their business. When they were finished with the 200 pounds of weed she took them out and bought them brand new Lincoln Continentals. Dameka's was sky blue and Danielle's was a dark navy. Everything was going according to plan, until the weed connect down in Miami got busted. Now Darlene had to change her route, she called one of her cousins out in Pittsburgh, who hooked her up with a new connect. Disembarking from the plane their cousin Renny was eagerly waiting for them in the Arrivals section. Since they hadn't seen each other in about three or four years, they were all so excited by the reunion.

"What's up girl?!" Dameka screamed as she dropped her bags and hugged her cousin.

"Damn, ya'll lookin' good! I guess the streets must be feedin' ya'll well." Renny said as she noticed how fine the three girls looked.

Glancing at Renny, Darlene knew that she had to help her cousin. The outfit that she had on was threadbare and ill fitting; her leather jacket was worn and cracked, not to mention her leather boots leaned to the side at the heels.

1962
"Hey Renny," Darlene shouted, excited to see her younger cousin.

Cook City Publishing

BY THE O.G. WISEMAN

"Hey girl," Renny responded, playing it cool as if she wasn't as excited as Darlene, Danielle and Dameka were to see her. Renny's mother was Ralph Sawyers the sister, since she had allowed Renny to come down to Cook City to spend the summer with the girls, they became close to each other. Being an only child, Renny had grown up in the streets of Pittsburgh dealing with any problem that she encountered on her own. Without a male figure in her life, she had to learn most things the hard way. Overall, she had learned from her experiences and was able to use life's lessons to her advantage.

"Go back in the room and put your bag away while I finish cookin'," Darlene smiled. "Dameka, show her where to put her stuff!"

"Girl, you getting, so big," Renny said to Dameka as she looked at how well shaped her little cousin's body had gotten. "You almost as big as me!"
Placing her hand on her hips, Dameka strutted back and forth, "I'm startin' to look good ain't I?"
Bursting into the small bedroom, Danielle plopped down on the little box spring bed, "How long you stayin' wit' us cuz?"

"I don't know. My mom said for a few weeks, but she might let me stay for the whole summer!"

"That'll be good if she do. You ain't been around us since ya'll came down to James' funeral."
That night the girls had so much fun. After making sure Danielle and Dameka were fast asleep in the bed and

ready for school the next day. Darlene and Renny went out for a little walk, Darlene wanted to show her some of the spots where a lot of the good looking guys hung out.

"Now, don't you go gettin' any ideas," Darlene joked, pointing her finger at Renny, "yo' momma told me to look after you, and that's just what I aim to do!" Renny smirked, "Girl, I'm just as old as you!" They laughed.

The next four weeks seemed to fly by, with only a couple weeks left to spend with her cousins, Renny didn't want to leave them, but in many ways, she missed the rugged streets of Pittsburgh. One night, while up real late watching the news, Renny heard Darlene downstairs arguing with some guy named Howard that she had gone out with.

"I had a nice time out wit' you tonight, but I didn't appreciate you feelin' all over me, Howard."

"Come on now girl! You know you like how I be touching you," Howard slurred, trying to rub Darlene's thigh.

"See! Now there you go again!"

"Naw, there you go tryin' to play hard to get! Come on and let's go upstairs and get nasty!"

"Upstairs?! Fool you ain't comin' up any stairs. What made you think I was gonna give you some pussy?"

"Oh, something goin' down! I done spent my last

Cook City Publishing

Cook City Publishing

nine dollars."

Realizing that her cousin Darlene was getting ready to get into something she might not be able to handle, Renny slid into her Bo-Bo's and grabbed the baseball bat that the girls kept behind the door in case of emergencies. Creeping down the stairs, she stood in the darkened doorway and bided her time.

"Alright Howard, it's time to go," Darlene declared, tired of arguing back and forth with the drunken, horny fool. "I got a lot of stuff to tend to tomorrow! I think it's best if you leave!"

"I ain't goin no where 'til you un-ass my nine dollars or give me nine dollars worth of pussy!" Howard strutted, grabbing Darlene by the arm. That was Renny's cue, stepping out of the darkness with the aluminum bat; she swung CRACK, catching Howard in the shoulder knocking him out of the doorway onto the pavement. Staring in shocked disbelief, Darlene stood there with her box-cutter in her hand, watching her cousin defend her honor.

"Nigga, didn't she say it was time for yo' fool ass to go? Renny shouted. She swung the bat, CRACK, CRACK, CRACK, hitting Howard twice in the leg and once in the arm.

"Now, get the fuck outta' here before I stick this bat up yo' ass!"

Scrambling to get away from the feisty broad with the aluminum bat, Howard made it to his feet and stumbled down the street. When Danielle and Dameka woke up

the next morning and heard about what had happened,
they fell out laughing. They laughed so hard that tears
came to their eyes.

*   *   *

"We can't hang around here all day; we got some
bizzness to take care of."
Renny lived in the projects on the southside of
Pittsburgh. The crib that she was staying in was just
as bare as the sister's weed spot back in Cook city. An
older model of a black and white GE television set,
mismatched pieces of furniture, a little stereo and a
small bed were all that furnished the place. Looking
around, Darlene was convinced that her cousin's
financial status was at the low end.
After they were there for about 45 minutes, this kat
named Jeff showed up, Renny talked with him for a
minute, then he and Darlene discussed their business.
When they were done, she was very pleased with what
he had to say.
"If you buy enough, I will make sure that the
product gets back to your city, personally."
"I need 250 pounds, if you can handle that."
she said, looking him square in the face to gauge his
reaction.
"I got you, sugar, and that's a promise. Ya'll must
be doin' big things out in Cook City. When ya'll get
back home, give me a call and your merchandise will

Cook City Publishing

be there shortly afterwards.

"My homeboy Flush will meet you down there and take care of everything."

"Ok, Daddy-O."

After Jeff's departure, the girls laughed and caught up on old times. "Girl, you might as well come back to Cook City and get down wit' us." Dee offered. "We could use the help. Plus, I know you could too."

"Yeah, we need another badass bitch to move all this shit we are about to get," Dameka insisted.

"I don't know," Renny said hesitantly. She liked it out in Pittsburgh, but she was also ready to do some new things; her money was definitely low.

She was a tall, thick, yellow broad with reddish hair. She had ass and tits for days and would fit right into the scheme of things. Danielle looked at her.

"Come on girl, it's been a long time since we all been together."

After some coaxing it was settled, she was part of team. Darlene explained the whole operation to her and she was ready to get down.

"This decision is gonna change your whole life."

"I'm wit' ya'll, Dee. Ya'll my family."

That night they packed all of Renny's stuff, and the next morning got on the plane and they headed back to Cook City.

QUEEN BEE

CHAPTER THREE

THE STREETS

FLUSH DELIVERED the 250 pounds of weed just like Jeff had promised. It was a batch of fine 'Columbian Gold' reefer. One joint would get five people high as a kite. Handling his business with Dee, Flush let her examine the merchandise while he quickly counted the money. Two hours later, he was back on the road. Dee and the girls went straight to work. Dameka and Danielle took Corey and Pharrel twenty pounds each, she also hit Rick Doggs, (a kat who she had started creeping around with) off with five pounds. He was breaking the joints down, making about $5,000 off each one.

Darlene and Renny hit the streets hard. She showed her cousin every happening spot in the city. Clover Leaf Lounge on the southside, to Charlie's and Ernie's Bar in the heart of uptown. A few different spots had opened up since the last time that Renny had been there, but

Cook City Publishing

Cook City Publishing

everything else was basically the same. Third and Sixth Streets were still the main strips, where it all went down. From 'Sixth and Hustlas Row, to the 'Third Street Hoe Stroll'. Fast money, bad bitches and fancy cars. After showing Renny all of the do's and don'ts of the streets, Darlene took her past the weed spot. She quickly caught on to the operation, so they left and went back to the Speakeasy. By the time they arrived, Danielle was back from making her runs. She had a nice little crowd in the spot too. Renny was amped up when she felt the vibe of the Speakeasy.

"Now this is the type of shit I like." She said this while walking around looking at the whole set up.

"If you like this shit, then you shouldn't have a problem helping Danielle hold this piece down," Darlene responded, "ain't no doubt in my mind that you can't make it happen."

When they were done downstairs, Darlene took Renny upstairs to the second floor and showed her all of the firepower they had.

"Pick what you want, but make sure you can handle it. This could be the difference between life and death."

The sawed-off, chrome, pump shotgun immediately caught Renny's eyes.

"This is a bad muthafucka' right here!" She screamed excitedly, as she picked the gun up and softly began to stroke it like a cat. "I damn near came all over myself." They both laughed.

Her second choice was a rubber-gripped, snub-nosed .357.

"Let one of these niggas act up and see what I give 'em! This bitch ain't to be fucked wit', and I ain't playin'!"

JUNIOR DENNISON was growing up fast. It seemed like he became a man overnight. One day, while Darlene and the rest of the girls were out getting their hustle on, this fat, nasty, short, dark-skinned nigga named Charlie C. tried to break into the speakeasy. Creeping up behind him, Junior startled Charlie C.

"If you don't sit yo' young ass down and stay outta grown folks business, I'ma give you what yo' daddy shoulda' gave ya" he hollered as he spun around to face Junior. With cat-like reflexes, Junior caught Charlie C. in the side of the head, WOP, and knocked him to the ground.

"You little muthafucka'!" he stammered, as he got up from his knees. "Now I'm gonna fuck yo' young ass up!"

Before Charlie C. could make it back up to his feet, Junior caught him again. This time a straight left jab, busting him in the mouth.

"I may be young, but I'm damn sure gonna kick yo' fat ass!"

Quicker then Junior could blink, Charlie C. kicked him in the chest and knocked him down. Before he could hit the ground, Charlie C. was on him. As they began to

Cook City Publishing

tussle, Junior pulled his snub-nosed .22 out of his back pocket. Charlie C.'s eyes got wider then the Grand Canyon. Pointing his pistol in Charlie's face, Junior roared.

"Now, I'm gonna give yo' punk-ass five seconds to run! After that, I'ma let this muthafucka' ring!" Charlie C. jumped up and darted. Before he could cut the corner, PAP, PAP, Junior shot him twice in the ass. The bullets didn't stop him; they just made him run faster.

"You punk-ass bitch!" Junior screamed, as he dusted off his clothes.

*   *   *

"Now this is what it is," Junior stared up at his father, listening very intently as he was being spoken to. "At this stage of your life, you might not be able to understand everything that I'm gonna say to you, but as much as you can, take it in and don't ever forget it! As you begin to grow up in this cold and twisted world, always remember as a man, to stand for something. Whatever sides of the street you decide to walk on, I want you to control it. You got your mother and me embedded in you, and I want you to always be a leader! Don't ever second-guess yourself or follow nobody. Since you been a baby, your mom and I taught you right from wrong, I expect you to be ten times the man that I

am. If you fail at something, I won't be mad at you. Just learn from your mistakes, and use the lessons as steps on your ladder to success!

As you begin to grow as a man, you will experience a lot of difficult things. I won't always be around, so you will have to handle your situations just as a real man would handle them! Do you understand?" Nine year old Junior Dennison took everything in that his father was telling him, and stored the information in the back of his mind. The jewels that he was being handed would become very valuable to him later on in his life. Removing a camel cigarette from his pack, Phillip lit one up and continued, "Life is surrounded by many temptations. As you are disciplined in certain areas, you will be able to withstand and control those inner cravings that often destroy a lot of powerful men! Whatever you do, I don't ever want you to allow a woman to control you or your destiny! If a woman is good, then treat her as such. Don't ever be fooled or misled by a nice body and a pretty smile. Chasing loose women will hold you back in many ways! You're the spitting image of me," Phillip laughed. "So, I know that the women are gonna be at you, boy! Just remember to think wit' ya' head, not the one in you pants. I hate to say it, but you were born into a certain type of life. You didn't ask to be born into it, but that's the way God made it! For whatever reason, you must make the best of it! You are a young prince right now, but one day you will be crowned 'King of

Cook City Publishing

BY THE O.G. WISEMAN

*Cook City'. I just hope that you will be able to handle
the reins. I've traveled many roads and ran through
many roadblocks, so I know first-hand what you gonna
be faced wit'. Don't ever allow yourself to fall weak
in the days when you are being tested, those are the
times when you will be measured for your true worth.
When you look into the mirror, you should be able to
look at your reflection with confidence. You can fool the
world most of the time, but you will never be able to
fool yourself. Just like building blocks must be put into
place one at a time, you must start with the cornerstone.
That's what I am, the cornerstone. Your mother is
the next block, and you follow her! Your name alone,
'Junior Dennison', is supreme, and will go a long way
in the future! I don't ever want you to do anything to
taint or distort it!"*

*Pulling out a large roll of hundred dollar bills, Phillip
showed one to his son, "This here rules the streets!
Don't ever let it rule you! Many people sell their souls
and lose their lives for this, and it ain't even worth the
paper it was printed on! It breaks up families, breaks
down friendships and destroys nations. It is said to
be the root of evil, but I say that the love of it is what
actually makes it evil! Money and drugs are a very
powerful combination. With them, kingdoms and
impenetrable fortresses are built! Many of the people
that circulate out in the streets either sell drugs or use
them. No matter which one of the two they do, their
lives are being affected by the decisions that they make.*

Your choices are very, very, very important! One wrong will cause a lot; maybe even a lifetime of pain. You follow me?"

"Uh-huh."

"You know your old man ain't gonna be around forever, don't you! If I do happen to pass on before you and ya' mother, you better do your best to take care of her! And always respect her. Lil' nigga, Dee is my queen, and you must always treat her as such."

Phillip squinted, changing his tone from subtle to just below a growl. "Everything I do is for ya'll. I know you are just a little boy right now, but you must pay close attention and observe everything that goes on around you. I don't want to put no pressure on you, but I want you to see how important the things that I'm saying' to you are!"

Grabbing his son by the shoulder, Phillip pulled him over to him and hugged him. "I love you, boy! Don't you ever forget that!" Willing the tears not to fall, Phillip left his son with one final jewel. "Always move in silence, and remember that the best kept secret goes to the grave wit' you!"

(Junior never told Darlene about what happened with Charlie C., he kept it to himself. If anything else ever jumped off, he would handle that too.)

*   *   *

Cook City Publishing

BY THE O.G. WISEMAN

Cook City Publishing

Darlene was spreading her wings. She was opening up spots in every part of town. Renny was her right hand, and she made sure that they ran like clockwork. With Renny in charge, the streets hardly ever saw Darlene, and that gave her some extra time. She visited Phillip's gravesite at least once or twice a week. She always brought flowers, and sat down to talk with him. The visits made her feel better. It had been awhile since Phillip's murder, and Darlene still hadn't allowed any man to get next to her. A few kats had tried, but she always checked them and put them in their place. Darlene still had Phillip's Cadillac, she always drove it. "Soon, I'm gonna buy me another car and park my baby in the garage," she told herself. She had put off buying herself a new car when Renny came back to Cook City with them. She laced her cousin with the same type of Lincoln that Dameka and Danielle had. Renny's car was pearl white with a white leather interior. On her license plate, she had 'G-B-3'. Dameka had 'G-B-1' and Danielle 'G-B-2'.

They all knew how to play, and they were playing the streets hard.

> *   *   *

DAMEKA AND PHARREL were laying their hustle down everywhere they went. Moving 25 to 30 pounds a week, it was strictly about money. The 'Colombian Gold' reefer that Darlene copped from Jeff had the street flying sideways. Anybody in the city that smoked weed either bought product from one of the girls, their soldiers or one of the people that bought their weed. Otto's Bar on Seventeenth and Market Streets was jumping on Friday night. Dameka and Pharrel came tippin' through. Dressed fresh ta' def in a brown ruffled-lace jumpsuit, knee-high brown leather boots and a matching brown leather jacket with a mink fur collar, Dameka looked sexier than Ayana Mitchell. Pharrel was dressed from head to toe in brown as well. Pimpin' a brown leather brim cocked to the side on his head, a brown and white silk pinstriped suite, with some brown patent leather floor shines on. Many people mistook him for a young Ike Turner.

Otto cracked a big smile when he saw Dameka and Pharrel. Looking over at Gus the bartender, he gave them a thumbs up. "What's up Daddy-O?" Dameka said, as he showed them to their table.

"I ain't makin' no calls right now," Otto slurred, "but I do wish I had something as sweet as you on my arms. I would stick her, flip her and lick her all the way up and down."

Looking at Otto with a boyish grin, Pharrel replied. "Shit nigga, if you had something this sweet, you'd probably O.D."

"I know that's right!" Dameka added. They laughed. Sitting at their table near the door, Pharrel and

BY THE O.G. WISEMAN

Dameka could see everything that came in the joint. Every hustla that came through stopped by to see if that 'Columbian Gold' was still poppin'. They always acknowledged Pharrel, but most of them wanted to see how good Dameka was looking. During the course of the night, they sold almost five pounds of weed. Pharrel was making the moves, but Dameka was giving the orders. She always allowed him to feel like he was in charge, but when it really came down to it, they both knew who the real boss was. Pharrel knew Darlene, but he never did any of his business with her. He hardly ever saw her, and he talked even less to her. He was satisfied with his role though, because he was making ten times more money now than before he had hooked up with Dameka.

Pharrel was a true hustla, he realized that the streets of Cook City were Darlene's and her clique's. Nobody else in the game was seeing as much money as they were, He didn't care what type of hustle they had going on, from one end of the city to the other end, from one block to the next, if it was some weed being sold, Darlene had her hands in it. But what made it so sweet was that she didn't have to touch a thing. She had three down-ass bitches, with game like Wilt Chamberlain, and a supporting championship cast. All she had to do was coach and Pharrel was happy to be on the team.

*   *   *

QUEEN BEE

THE HOLIDAY Inn suite was the scene. Danielle was waiting in Room 503 for Rick Doggs to arrive. They had some business to handle, both financial and sexual. In her overnight Jordache bag sitting next to the dresser, she had a one-piece orange mini-dress, some white crotchless panties, a pair of white high-heeled pumps, and seven pounds of weed. Rick Doggs had finished with the other package that he had, and now she was giving him more…much. Answering the door when he arrived, Danielle was wrapped in nothing but a pink towel. As he embraced her, she allowed it to fall to the floor. Slowly caressing and rubbing her ass, he looked down at her breasts, and then walked over to the bed and sat down.

Danielle met Richard Lemberk, a.k.a. Rick Doggs, at Gino's Restaurant up at Sixth and Division Streets…

A few weeks after his arrival in Cook City, from East New York. Taking his show on the road, Rick Doggs was looking to step his hustle up. Being a true 'jack-of-many-trades' at a young age, he could switch his pitch up whenever he chose to. During the short span that he had been in the game, he had adopted and played many roles, gun-toter, scam artist, stick-up kid, and finally full fledged hustla.

Moving through the grimy streets of Brooklyn with a chip on his shoulder, no father or mother, only hunger for a mentor and bloody eyes as a guide, he was

Cook City Publishing

dangerous in every way. Being persecuted by the police and hunted by many of the people he had either shot or robbed, he got wind of the capital of Pennsylvania and set his sails for Cook City.

"Damn ma! You the baddest thing I seen since Etta James!" Rick Doggs smiled at Danielle as he stopped in front of her table. "You mind if I sit and talk wit' you for a few minutes?"
Looking up at the attractive young kat, who obviously wasn't from Cook City, and had no idea of who she was, Danielle grabbed her napkin and wiped her mouth. "You sure this is where you wanna sit?"
"Ain't no doubt in my mind I'm tryna sit wit' you, ma!"
"Alright then, be my guest."
After paying for his food and returning to the table with his tray, Rick Doggs slid into the booth across from Danielle. "I don't mean to be too aggressive, but I like what I see, and I'm tryna have it. I hope I'm not offending you."
"Nah, young playa, it's cool. If you were, you can best believe that I would let you know."
"That's what's up. Now that we're pass that, my name is Rick Doggs."
"Hi Rick, my name is Danielle. Hearing you speak, and lookin' at how you are dressed, I can tell you ain't from around here. You sound like you from New York or New Jersey."

Rick Doggs smiled, "I'm from East New York, momma.
I see you can detect certain lingos."
Realizing that the young, good-looking kat sitting across
from her was new to the city, Danielle studied Rick
Doggs for a few moments before speaking.

"So, what brought you to Cook City, Rick Doggs?"
she inquired, scrutinizing his facial expressions as she
waited for his answer.

"On the up, I came here to see what type of paper
these streets be generating." That was all Danielle
needed to hear, "You sure this is the right spot for
you?"

"I heard about Cook City from my people up top,
and they told me that if I laid my game down correctly, I
could live real comfortable down here.

"You know anybody around here?"

"Well, met a couple of kats, and a few different
broads, but other than that, I ain't really tryin' to meet
too many people, unless it's about some paper."

"Oh yeah?"

"I know you dig me."

Danielle was impressed by many of Rick Doggs answers.
The more they talked, the more she could picture him
fitting into the scheme of things.

"Enough questions about me, Sugar," Rick Doggs
said, flipping the conversation. "What's up wit' you?
You got a man?"

"A man?" Danielle smiled. "What are you askin'
me something like that for? I gotta be at least several

years older than you are."

"And?"

"And, that means you ain't ready for the major league. You might be from New York and all, but what I'm playin' wit' is much bigger than that."

"The major league?" Rick Doggs was puzzled by the fine broad's confident statement. He could tell there was much more to the statement than met the eyes. "So, how old are you, sweetie?"

"That doesn't matter right now," Danielle replied, skirting the question. "You just better be ready for what you tryin' to get ya'self into."

"Oh, I'm ready!"

Fifteen minutes later, Danielle was taking Rick Doggs on a ride that would change the rest of both of their lives.

"Here goes that money, sweetheart. You always taught me that it was bizness before pleasure." Pulling $4,400 out of his pocket, he sat the money down on the nightstand, and turned his back to her.

"I see you been handlin' ya' bizness." Danielle said in a sexy tone of voice, walking over to the bed, looking down into Rick Doggs emerald green eyes. "Now that the bizness part is over, let's have some pleasure."

Danielle was an old head and she knew exactly how to pleasure her young boy. Pushing him back on the bed, she slowly unzipped his pants "Close your eyes baby. Let me show you how good I can make you feel."

The moistness of her lips and tongue felt like a wet pussy, as she professionally started to suck and lick his dick. Instantly she brought Rick Doggs to a climax.

"Let it all go." she groaned, while sucking the last drop of semen out of his dick. Quickly she undressed him and got him hard again. As she mounted him, Rick Doggs grabbed her hips and pressed hard inside of her.

"Oohhhhh!" she screamed, as he continued thrusting inside of her. "Yes…do it harder baby!" Seconds later, she reached her peak. Pulling Danielle over to the edge of the bed, Rick Doggs stood over her, and pushed both of her legs back as far as they would go. Entering inside of her, his pleasure seemed immeasurable. Harder and harder, he began to stroke grabbing the sheets and gasping for air, it became difficult for her to breathe. As beads of sweat rolled down Rick Doggs forehead and back, he took one final stroke. Releasing himself like a breath of fresh air, he left Danielle caught up in another moment of climatic rapture. Trembling, shaking and panting for more.

*   *   *

RENNY WAS CATCHING on fast. She was bringing in much more money than Dee had expected her to. She could run the Speakeasy and the weed spots with both of her eyes closed. With one hand on her hip and one hand on her clip, she wouldn't hesitate to put a lame on his back. Standing out in front of the weed spot on Emerald Street, she ran into this junkie named Blue Notes.

"I'm tryin' to get a job lil' momma. Why don't you help me out?" he asked, while scratching the left side of his face. Analyzing him, her antennas went up.

"Nigga you betta' not be tryin' to get over on me? The last thing you want is me on yo' ass!"

"Naw! Naw! Baby girl, I'm being straight up. I'm tryin' to get money."

"What type of money you tryna get?"

"I'm tryin' to get that supreme money. You already know that triple beam money. If I'm lyin', I'm flyin'."

"Naw nigga, if you lyin', you dyin'."

Later that evening, Renny hit Blue Notes off with a pound of weed.

Six days later, she ran up on him standing down on the corner of Jefferson and Woodbine Streets in a deep nod. She pulled her car over and crept up on him.

"You think I'm a muthafuckin' joke or somethin', don't you, nigga!" she shouted, throwing the barrel of her pump shotgun in his face. The rest of the dope fiends and junkies that were gathered around scattered and cleared the corner. The only two people left were Blue Notes and Renny.

"Wait, wait, wait, wait a minute baby doll, I been

Cook City Publishing

lookin' for you for damn near a week!" he stuttered in between nods. The bogus words made Renny even madder then she already was. Shoving the barrel of the shotgun in Blue Notes' mouth, she cocked the pump, CLICK! CLACK!

"Get yo' bitch ass down on ya' knees!"

"Come on Renny, this shit ain't that serious."

"What, nigga? My money is always serious." she said as she smacked him in the face with the butt of the gun. Blood came streaming down his nose, as he fell backwards to the ground. Renny let three shots loose down at the pavement, right next to where Blue Notes was laying. Scared to death, his bowels came loose and he shit all over himself.

"I'ma, give ya trick ass until tomorrow night to get my muthafuckin' money right, sissy! If you don't get it, then you gonna get it, you lame ass nigga!" Slowly backing away with the pump still aimed at him, she got back into the car, rolled down the window, and let off several more shots. The night turned silent as she rode away.

*   *   *

JUNIOR AND DARLENE got up early Sunday morning and went to church. They hadn't been there in a while. The last time that either of them had attended a service, Phillip was alive. Darlene and Junior spent that whole day together. After leaving church, they went by the graveyard to visit Phillip, and placed some flowers on his headstone. Returning back home from a day full of enjoyment, they ate dinner, watched television, and then Junior went upstairs and got ready for bed. Darlene loved her son, and she always wanted him to know that. Any and every chance she got she never failed to show him how much he really meant to her.

*   *   *

"YO, YO, YO! Did you hear about them four badass bitties from Uptown?" Donnie Danz said, sitting back in the corner of Henderson's bar sipping on a cold glass of Thunderbird on the rocks. "I heard them broads is about they business!"
Dressed down in a money green Paul Smithy suit, a velour hat, and a pair of money green 'gators, Fred Johnson replied, "Dee Dennison and her crew!"
"I don't know names, nigga! All I know is that it's supposed to be four of the finest skins in Cook City!"
"If they from Uptown, then you gotta' be talkin' about Dee and 'em. Matter of fact, if you talkin' 'bout four broads period, that's about they business, then you talkin' 'bout Dee and 'em!"
"Nigga, how you know?" Donnie Danz reared back in his chair and downed the rest of his drink.
"Nigga, I knew Dee's husband, Phillip!"

"You talkin' about Phillip that got murdered up around Jefferson Street?"

"Yeah nigga! That's the Phillip I'm talkin' 'bout!"

"I knew Phillip too!"

"Nigga, you ain't know Phillip Dennison!"

"Man, I used to get pounds of weed off that nigga! He was from down in Miami."

Fred smiled, knowing that Donnie Danz knew who Phillip was. "That was my muthfuckin' nigga! If it was goin' down, this nigga was gettin' it over wit'! Phillip ain't take no shit! He was a respectable type nigga, but if you got on his bad side, he was for sure to put somethin' hot in yo' ass."

"Yo, that nigga had the jumpin' ass Speakeasy too!"

"That joint is still open!"

"Stop playin', nigga!"

"I ain't playin! Them four broads you talkin' 'bout be runnin' that spot! They still got the weed jumpin' off, too."

Fred paused for a minute, lit up a cigarette, and then continued, "Nigga, how you know Phillip and don't know who Dee is?"

"I don't know, baby! I guess I just got in and got out when I went up to the spot."

Fred laughed. "That mighta' been a good thing, you might not be here talkin' shit right now."

A few people who were scattered around the small bar chuckled. Standing up, Donnie Danz strolled over to the

Cook City Publishing

jukebox.

"That nigga Phillip must'a laid his game down strong, he been gone for a minute, and four broads is still carrying his legacy on."

"That's what type of nigga he was." Fred declared. "He was real wit' everything he did."

"Man, I don't know which one of them broads it was, but word on the street is that she shook Blue Notes' ass up!"

"Yeah, I heard about that too. That's Dee's cousin Renny! She supposed to be from Pittsburgh. They say she got a happy trigger-finger that loves to laugh. If you see her, you would never know that she was a real rough type of broad. Chick look like somethin' you wanna take home and spend the rest of ya life in the bed wit'."

"It's like that?"

"You gotta see for ya'self, pimp daddy. Dee got two badass sisters too, all of them top stock."

"I keep hearin' niggas talkin' 'bout 'em, but I thought it was all hype!"

"Ain't nothin' hype 'bout this." Fred raised his eyebrows. " All one million proof, baby!"

"One million, playa?"

"One million, Daddy-O, like a nigga hit the lottery! You gotta see for ya'self. Make sure you be real easy when you do, I don't wanna' be readin' about yo' ass in the obituaries."

QUEEN BEE

*   *   *

RENNY'S NAME was blazing like wild fire in Cook City. When it came down to the money stacks, she let the streets and every nigga that was in them know 'what it was hittin' for'. If it was love, then it was love; but there was no such thing as love in the streets that she ran in. You can love the streets but the streets won't love you back.

Meandering through Time Hotel and Bar out on the Hillside part of town, Renny ran into this smooth-ass pimp named Base. When they first crossed paths, she knew that it was on. Decked out in a light tan leather jumpsuit, and a pair of caramel colored suede boots, Renny was sharper than a razor. You could see every curve of her body.

"That must be jelly, cause jam sho' don't shake like that." Base said as he slid up to her in a lavender tailor-made suit, with his light brown hair waved to the back.

"What's yo' name cutiepie? I'm Base, but all my hoes call me 'Big Daddy.'"

Tickled and amused, Renny responded, "What's up playa, my name is Renny. If you buyin', I'm drinkin'."

"For you, lil' mamma, I'll buy the bar out. Let's get tipsy in the muthafucka."

Cook City Publishing

BY THE O.G. WISEMAN

Cook City Publishing

A half hour later, Renny had Base all figured out. '*I don't know how this nigga became a pimp,*' she thought to herself. "These must be some weak-ass hoes out here."

Digging Renny's style, Base drank and danced the whole night. Base gave her all of his attention, he damn near forgot about all of his hoes. Interruptions from them made him mad. "What the fuck do ya'll keep botherin' me for? I know ya'll see me in the middle of somethin'. Ya'll better have my muthafuckin' money right!" he snapped.

Renny just smiled and acted as if she hadn't heard the way he talked to the other women who approached him. In fact, she was more amused at the thought of doing what she had planned.

At 2:30 a.m., just as the club was closing, Base gathered up all of his hoes. "I'm about to go handle some bizness," he said, as he peered over at Renny's sexy ass waiting for him in her car. "If I come back, and you bitches ain't got my money right, somebody is gonna get my foot planted upside they muthafuckin' head!"

Tonya, Pamela, Trixie, Lisa and Gracie all listened and gave Base their full attention, knowing full well what would happen to them if they ever fucked up. Base and Renny left and went straight to the Reilly Street Hotel. As he was paying for the room, she peeked to see what type of bankroll her was rolling with and was actually kind of impressed. Up in the secondhand rundown ghetto suite, with just a nightstand, lamp and outdated

QUEEN BEE

Zenith 21" colored television and a lumpy queen-sized bed, Renny threw the pussy straight on Base, turning the game up to the next level. She knew that he was used to having his hoes do whatever he wanted them to do, but tonight, he was going to do things her way. Renny had Base's balls in her hands, and his dick in her mouth, driving him crazy. Gently massaging his genitals and blowing his socks off, suddenly she stopped. Renny looked up at him, licked her luscious lips nice and slowly, and laughed.

"My pussy is achin' nigga, it needs to be soothed. Show me how good you can work that tongue."
With no hesitation, Base jumped in the pussy, face first; his tongue was like a whip. He made Renny cum, cum, cum, and cum again, never wasting a drop of her tasty white juices. Satisfied with Base's work, Renny finished her job, sucking him as dry as the Sahara Desert. Base was sprung! After Renny took a shower, she began to get dressed.

"Where you goin' baby?" he asked as he rose from the bed with a pleading look on his face.

"I got some money to get." Renny responded. "I sure ain't gettin' none here."

"Come on now, sugar, don't go."

"It's been fun, but I gotta run playa."
Base jumped up, pulled his bankroll out of his pocket and tried to hand it to her. Renny laughed. "I know you got more than this, if you wanna be wit' me, then you got to be able to take care of me. I ain't no low class

Cook City Publishing

hoe, nigga."

"What is it you want, baby?" Base pleaded as he sat back down on the bed and reached out to her. Renny laid the law down to him strong and hard, when she was done explaining the situation to him she had Base wrapped around her middle finger. Base was willing to do whatever was necessary to be part of her life. Base was definitely 'Big Pimpin' them hoes out in the street, but that night, Renny pimped the shit out of him.

Cook City Publishing

CHAPTER FOUR

THE QUEEN

"I'M GOING up to New York for a couple of days. I wanna get away and clear my mind." Darlene said as she, Renny, Danielle and Dameka sat in the living room talking. "I know that ya'll are gonna be able to hold it down while I'm gone. I don't feel that I need to tell ya'll what to do or how to do it, ya'll already know. The most important thing that I want ya'll to do is take care of Junior."

Everything had been going just the way that Darlene had been envisioning it, but she was beginning to feel that another step towards success had to be taken. She was conscious of finding new ways to enhance her hustle. She knew that to be a good leader, she had to be able to dissect and breakdown her thoughts and deal with each one according to its importance. Phillip had left her many jewels, all of which were very valuable.

BY THE O.G. WISEMAN

Cook City Publishing

"I'm sorry you had to see me act up on that nigga Roy, the other night, but baby." Phillip apologized to Darlene, sitting at the edge of their bed massaging her feet. *"That fool put me in a situation! I gave him a chance to make it right, but he insisted on gettin' over like a fat rat. Before I reacted to what he had done, I thought for a few moments and weighed my options. I knew I couldn't let him get away wit' what he was tryin' to pull off. If I did that, how many other niggas you think would'a tried to follow and dress up in the same suit! I didn't wanna do that to Roy, but he left me wit' no choice. See, baby, what I do is for you and Junior, if a nigga try to disturb that, then I gotta do whatever it is that I gotta do to make sure that he don't succeed in his ploy."*

Absorbed in the feeling of Phillip's soft hands caressing her feet, Darlene laid back on the bed with her eyes closed and her ears wide open.

"I can't speak on tomorrow, because it has not arrived yet. I can only make plans for a better one," Phillip continued; *"but if I fail to plan properly, failing to look at life from every possible angle, then I know that what I am tryin' to accomplish will never be obtained. It is only when I look at things in their entirety that I can place everything in its proper order. Without order there is no real formation, and without true vision, dreams can never be manifested. One of the craziest things in the world is when a dog chases its own tail. That's what happens to us when we allow ourselves to*

become caught up in the streets and we begin to chase after things that are virtually meaningless. I want you to know that you are what brings meaning to my life. You keep my fire burning, and my ambition at its highest level. I don't know what it is, but for some reason, I feel that I ain't gonna be around for too much longer."
Stung by Phillip's last statement, Darlene opened her eyes and sat up "Don't talk like that baby. You scarin' me!"

"I don't ever speak to scare you, Dee! I speak to make you aware and to try and help you understand what life is really all about. When I'm gone, you gonna have to carry on. The torch must never be on low, you gotta keep it blazin'! Junior is gonna depend on you, and you must be able to give him the guidance that he will need to keep him focused in a world of illusions."
Becoming emotionally stirred, Darlene began to cry, "Why you talkin' like this, Phillip?"
Gazing deeply into Darlene's eyes, Phillip placed her face inside of his hands and softly kissed her on the lips.

"DO YA' THANG GIRL!" Renny replied. "You don't have to think twice about us handling our bizness."

"We like glue, baby girl, we always gonna stick together." Dameka said.

"One for all, and all for one." Danielle added.

"I will holla at ya'll in a minute." Pulling her brand new powder blue Cadillac El Dorado out of the garage, Darlene hit the highway.

At 4:00 a.m. the next morning, she checked into the Econo Suites in Center City, Manhattan. After a short nap and a light breakfast, she went out. Cruising through the New York streets seemed to expand her mind. The feeling of the big city was quite different from that of Cook City. Making her way through the New York City traffic jams, Darlene rode up to 42nd Street and then went over to Central Park. She took pictures of the Empire State Building, and rode the ferry to Ellis Island for a tour of the Statue of Liberty. Returning to Manhattan, she ate lunch at a fancy restaurant down in Times Square. In the mood for a little shopping, Darlene went over to Canal Street to buy a couple of pieces of Jewelry. She bought four pairs of gold diamond encrusted earrings for her and her girls. Then she walked across the street and copped a three-karat diamond ring for herself. Before she left the jewelry store, she bought Junior a solid gold rope chain with a diamond pendant on it.

Macy's was Darlene's final stop on her shopping spree. She was on her way into the department store, when she ran straight into this tall, thick bronze-skinned chick coming out of the door with an armful of shopping bags. The collision knocked all of the girl's bags to the ground.

"Excuse me." Darlene said as she bent down to help pick up the scattered packages.

"Oh, that's all right, I should have been lookin' where I was goin' myself." the girl replied. Standing back up, Darlene noticed how fly the outfit was that the girl had on.

"Did you buy that skirt outta here?"

"No, I got this from over on Delancey Street. You ain't from around here, are you?"

"I'm from Cook City, Pennsylvania." Darlene answered. "What's ya name, girl?"

"I'm Coochie from Brownsville. If you want, I can help you find some nice outfits after I take these bags to the car."

For the rest of the day, Darlene and Coochie went splurging. When they were done, Darlene was dead tired. Before going back to her hotel room, Darlene gave Coochie her phone number.

"Call me later on, girl so that we can go out and have a little bit of fun. I ain't lookin' for no man, I wanna see what the clubs are hittin' fo'."

"I'm wit' that," Coochie replied.

Three hours later, Coochie was at Darlene's hotel room. She was dressed so live that she could have brought Louis Armstrong back from the grave. She had on a cream colored knee-length one-piece dress, with blue and orange peacock feathers around the sleeves. The bodice of the dress had a plunging neckline that amply displayed her cleavage; a serious eye-catching effect. Her beige high-heeled shoes, with wrap-around ankle

Cook City Publishing

Cook City Publishing

straps, were beyond sexy. Her sandy hair was blown out into a small but sassy afro. As Coochie stepped through the door, Darlene gave her a definite look of approval.

"Go ahead, wit' yo' badass self!"
Coochie spun around and did a little dip. Feeling herself, she examined what Darlene had on. Midnight blue was Darlene's choice of color for the night. The body hugging skirt suit she was wearing had a split up the back that stopped just below her ass. The white blouse and buckled down white pumps that she had on complimented the white turban she was sporting. Her persona was definitely that of a classy bitch, and she carried herself just as that. She knew that her outfit was saying something, and her walk said it all.

"Damn, sugar, you sure did put that shit together. I'ma have to go back and get me one of them sets." Coochie complimented, as she winked at her friend. After Darlene grabbed her pocketbook, they both took one final look in the mirror and then left. Coochie took Darlene up to a nice little spot in Harlem. Entering the club, Darlene could tell that this was a place where a lot of money circulated. Everyone from the bouncers to the bartender were dressed superbly in custom fitted suits. The tables were decorated with candles and roses. The two-leveled dance floor was arrayed with colorful disco lights. The thick red carpeting that covered the VIP section made its occupants feel more relaxed.

"What's up Bino?" Coochie greeted the big black, muscular kat at the door. "Where's Mission?"

Without uttering a single word, Bino pointed them to a booth near the stage. Reaching the booth, Coochie introduced Darlene to this dark-skinned, handsome looking guy with long braids reaching down to the middle of his back.

"Dee, this is Mission. Mish, this is my friend Dee from Cook City."

"I'm delighted to meet you Dee. I must say that you are a very attractive woman."

"Thank you."

"May I order you two beautiful ladies something to drink?"

"Sure, why not?" Darlene answered. "I will have a tall glass of ripple on the rocks."

"You already know what I'm drinking." Coochie stated. While waiting for the waitress to return with their drinks, Mission and Coochie went to the dance floor to get their groove on. Darlene was enjoying the scene and jamming to the music when this tall, attractive kat with an afro walked over to their table.

"I couldn't help but notice that the finest chick in this club was sittin' over here by herself, so I had to come over and say something to you."
Flattered by the compliment, Darlene listened as he tried to lay his game down. After exchanging names, they got up and danced. It had been a long time since Darlene danced and she felt self-conscious and funny. The D.J. was playing the new Stevie Wonder joint. The whole club was bouncing and grooving. The dance

floor was overflowing with diddy boppers. When the song ended, Darlene thanked Pauley for the dance and then, went back to the table and sat with Coochie and Mission. As Darlene was settling in her seat, Mission stood up. "Excuse me ladies, I will be right back, I have an important phone call to make." he said before leaving them. Seconds after his departure, Darlene inquired, "Girl, is that yo' man?"

"More like my ex-man." Coochie laughed. "He had too many hoes for me. We ain't together no more, but we're still friends. You already know how that goes, when a nigga get a lil' bit of money, every bitch in town wanna give him a piece of ass."
Darlene looked at her and raised her glass, "I know that's right."

When Mission returned to the table, Darlene examined him closely. She analyzed his whole style and concluded that he was a major playa in the streets of New York. For the rest of the night, Darlene and Coochie had a ball. At 4:30 a.m. they left the club. On their way back to Darlene's room she said, "Cooch, you might as well use that other bed that I got. It's kind of late for you to be out here by ya'self."
Thinking about the drive back to Brooklyn, Coochie agreed. "Okay, girl, I'm tired as a muthafucka anyway."

*   *   *

QUEEN BEE

LEANING UP against the phone booth at Third and MacLay Streets, Rick Doggs looked up the hill and noticed Peon strolling his way with a mean hook in his arm. 'This nigga,' he laughed to himself. "Rick Doggs, what it be like, playa?" Peon grinned, sliding up on him, shaking his hand.

"You already know, Daddy-O! Plenty of cash, that grass and an occasional shot of ass!" They laughed.

"You got that for me?" Peon asked, glancing around in a paranoid motion.

"Now, if I didn't have what you needed, you think I would be down on this damn corner waiting for ya' ass, nigga?"

"I'm just checkin', baby." Peon tried to assure Rick Doggs.

"Hey Doggs, I need to handle what we need to handle so I can take care of some other business."

"I got you, playa! Just give me a minute, I'm waiting on this phone call so…" The phone rings. Stepping inside of the phone booth, Rick Doggs slid the door closed behind him and picked up the phone. A few minutes later, he came back out with a smile on his face.

"Let's go handle that!"

"How far we gotta' go?" Peon asked impatiently.

"Damn, nigga! You must be in a real hurry." Rick Doggs responded irritably. "You need to slow the fuck down. I got you right here in my book bag. You got all the money, don't you? This pound of grass ain't goin' for nothin' less than what it's supposed to go for."

BY THE O.G. WISEMAN

A car full of girls blew at Rick Doggs as they rode down Third Street. Glancing to see who his passing admirers were, he took his eyes off of Peon for a brief moment. When he turned his attention back, the 6'3 light-skinned kat with a baldhead was pointing a snub-nosed revolver at him.

Cook City Publishing

"I ain't got the money, cool breeze, but I do got this! You ain't got no business down here in Cook City anyway, nigga! Un-ass that, fat rat!"
Rick Doggs couldn't believe Peon was trying to jerk him, but then again, he could. From the time that Peon had walked up on the corner, he could feel that something wasn't right.

"It ain't worth it Peon man, I'm tellin' you! Rick Doggs tried to warn him. "This bullet you 'bout to bite is real bitter!"
Peon laughed. "Nigga, I'm the one with the gun! You might be the one bitin' the muthafuckin' bullet, Flea. Now give that shit up!" Handing Peon the bag, Rick Doggs shook his head. "Smart move." Peon snapped, backing away with the revolver in his hand.
Just as he turned to run down the dark vacant street, Rick Doggs pulled a chrome .44 magnum from up under his gray sweatsuit and squeezed the trigger. The first shot missed Peon, zipping past his head. The second slug caught him in the right side of his hip and knocked him into a parked car.

"AAAAAAHHHH! Oh shit!" Peon screamed like a hoe with a yard full of dick up inside of her. Laying on the ground, grabbing for his now missing hip, he was confused about what had just happened. Walking up on the wounded fool, who was squirming around like a fish fresh out of water, Rick Doggs pointed his gun down at Peon.

"I told you it wasn't worth it, nigga! Now bite this!" BOOM!

*   *   *

DARLENE AND COOCHIE both woke up around noontime. Ordering lunch from room service, they watched 'The Young and The Restless' and talked. As their conversation progressed, Darlene told Coochie what types of things she was into and why. Coochie was a down-ass chick from the heart of the slums. Going through her fair share of trials and tribulations, she had dibbled and dabbled in the game as well. Since the early age of 14, she had been on her own. Raising herself, she knew a lot about the streets.

"I need you to hook me up with Mission," Darlene said. "I peeped him out last night, and I know he is connected."

Surprised, Coochie looked up from the t.v., "You definitely know ya' shit, girl. I will talk to him later on and see what's up. Whatever you tryin' to get, he can get it."

Later that evening, Coochie called Darlene and told her

that Mission said that everything was good. At 9:00 p.m. that night, Darlene, Mission and Coochie met at her hotel suite. Without any small talk, Darlene got straight to the point.

"I appreciate you agreeing to meet me, and I am more than sure that this will be well worth your while. Right now I am trying to get three hundred pounds of some good weed." Caught off guard by such a request, Mission raised his eyebrows. Darlene continued, "I'm about my bizness and I don't play no games. I got money to get and moves to make."

"It won't be a problem getting that for you, Dee", Mission responded. "I will help you with this matter, but my line of work is cocaine. I am a businessman and therefore, we will conduct business."
After a price had been agreed upon and everything was finalized, Mission left. Darlene and Coochie sat in the suite and talked until the wee hours of the next morning. With all of her bags packed, Darlene was ready to go.

"I'ma give you a call in a couple of weeks girl. Take care of yourself, and tell Mission to have that shit ready for me."
Although Coochie had just met Darlene, she felt an almost instant sense of profound closeness to this Cook City sistah. She felt as though she had known Darlene all her life. Strangely, deep inside, it hurt Coochie to see Darlene leave. Hugging Darlene, she had to restrain herself from crying. "You take care of yourself too."
Before leaving New York, Darlene stopped over at Val's

Beauty Salon on 54th Street to get her hair done up. The blonde baby blowout gave her a whole new look, and it fitted her to a "T". She was Cook City's baddest B.I.T.C.H., in the flyest way, and couldn't nobody deny it. On her way back home, Darlene felt better, and much more confident. She could feel that her money stacks were on the rise. Junior and Darlene started spending a lot more quality time together.

After returning home, she spent almost everyday for the next two weeks with him. They went skating, to the movies, bowling and even to the Isley Brothers concert at the Forum. Darlene knew that Junior was getting older, and she encouraged him to get good grades in school. When he brought his report card with second honors on it, she took him out to the motorcycle shop and bought him a brand new Honda mini-bike.

"Your father would be very proud of you. You already know what type of man he wanted you to grow up to be, and I know that he is smiling right now." Darlene told Junior as she hugged him fiercely and kissed him on the cheek. Junior was growing up, and growing up fast.

*   *   *

TWO DAYS LATER, Darlene made the call. Mission and Coochie fell through Cook City with 300 pounds of 'Mexican Red-Bud'. At the same time, Flush dropped

Cook City Publishing

off 300 pounds as well, giving Darlene and the girls 600 pounds of product to work with. Dameka and Renny handled the business with Flush, while Darlene met with Mission and Coochie.

"What's poppin' playa," Dameka said to Flush as he pulled up to the house in a brown customized van, with secret panels installed all over it.

"Ya'll already know. If it ain't about the money, then it ain't about shit." Renny smiled at him and licked her lips. Faster than he arrived, Flush left.

"Hey girl!" Darlene screamed as she and Coochie embraced.

"What it be like, baby girl?" Coochie responded.

"This is my sister Danielle. Danielle, this is Mission and Coochie."
Danielle had never met Coochie or Mission and, naturally, she had her defenses on alert. For some reason, she was fiending for something to jump off. She had her nickelplated .44 cocked and ready to blow inside her pocketbook. "I really like this little city of yours Dee." Mission said as he nodded his head. "It seems to be treating you very well."

"I make the best of it. On the real, I wouldn't have it any other way."
The transaction between Mission and Darlene went well, and Danielle was glad. As Mission and Coochie were getting ready to get back on the highway, Darlene grabbed Coochie's hand and said, "Cooch, I know ya' gonna spend a couple of days with me and my family.

I want you to meet my other sister, Dameka, and my cousin Renny. Plus, I wanna show you how we get down in Cook City."

Wanting to take Darlene up on her offer, but not wanting to seem too anxious, Coochie hedged. "I don't know, girl. I ain't really been outta New York." After talking it over for minute, Coochie decided to stay for about a week. Before Mission left, he gave Coochie $5,000 to have while she was in cook city.

"Call me if you need anything else, and keep that thing tight for Daddy."

"You be cool, playa." Darlene said as she winked at him. Then, Mission broke out. When Dameka and Renny got back from handling their business with Flush, Darlene introduced Coochie to the rest of her gang. Before Coochie arrived in Cook City, Darlene had already planned on asking her to become a part of her team. Now it was time. Darlene dug Coochie's style. She was almost eight years younger than Darlene was, but Darlene knew that she would fit into the scheme of things perfectly.

"Before I go any further," Darlene began, as she looked Coochie in the eye, "I have an important proposition for you." Puzzled, Coochie inquired, "What's the deal, Dee?"

"I have been thinking about this ever since I got back from New York, and now you are here. I wanna know if you wanna be a part of what we got goin' on?" Dameka, Danielle and Renny looked at one another in surprise. Darlene had told them about Coochie, but they had never expected anything like this. Coochie was surprised as well, and she really didn't know what to say. "Give me a couple of days to see if I feel this city, then I will give ya'll my answer."

"That's cool." Renny said. "After a couple of days you won't wanna go back home." They all laughed, and then got down to business. Darlene gave Dameka, Danielle and Renny 150 pounds apiece. That left her with 150 pounds for herself, when they were done discussing how it was going to be broken down, everybody went out and handled their business.

"Coochie, I want you to ride wit' Renny for a while, so she can show you how she moves on the streets. I will see you when ya'll get back, and then you and me gonna do some hangin'."
Coochie was more like Renny, and Darlene knew that they would click together. While Renny and Coochie were out, Renny showed her exactly what Darlene had shown her the first time around.

"You must be a slick-ass bitch for my cousin Darlene to wanna put you down with the clique. She's about her bizness, and she don't fuck around wit' no lame-ass tricks."

"I'm about my bizness too." Coochie stated. "I guess that's why she's feelin' me."
Before going back to the house, Renny told Coochie that she had to make one more stop. Pulling up on Third and Broad Streets, Renny parked the car and got

out. This slick-ass nigga in a tan suit, brown velour
hat and a pair of brown leather boots slid up on her,
kissed her hard and gave her a roll of money. Renny
whispered something is his ear, walked back to the car,
dropped a big green garbage bag out on the ground and
then pulled off.

"Who the fuck was that?" Coochie asked
excitedly.

"Oh, that nigga, he supposed to be a pimp. He got
a stable of hoes gettin' money for him, and he giving
half of it to me! Plus, he be movin' about fifteen to
twenty pounds a week for us. I might let him stroke this
kitten every now and then, and that's all it takes. Now,
you tell me, who's the muthafuckin' pimp!"
Cooch laughed. She was very impressed with the
way that Renny was putting it down. She saw Renny
make $10,000 in less then a couple of hours, not even,
counting that bankroll that she got from that trick-ass
pimp.

That night Darlene and Coochie went to Abe's Tavern
on Seneca Street. The small bar was standing room
only. Most of the big time playas, pimps and hustlas
hung out there, but when Darlene and her new protégé
came through the door, the whole scene changed.
Dressed in a black leather skirt, a gold leather and
suede tie-up vest, and a pair of gold 6" heeled leather
boots, Darlene had them looking.
Closely behind her, decked out in a leather skirt,
crochet top, and knee-high, open-toed leather boots,

Cook City Publishing

BY THE O.G. WISEMAN

Cook City Publishing

Coochie looked like Sincerely Ward. Jo-Jo the bartender laid it out for them. The whole night they drank free. Didn't a nigga come through the door that didn't come pay his respects to Darlene. What took the cake was when Jimmy Sharp played himself and tried to holla at Darlene.

"Nigga, if you don't carry yo' lame ass outta here, and come wit' some better game than that, I'ma put something in you!"

"Damn, it's like that, Dee?"

"Yeah. It's like that, nigga."

With his head hung low and his tail between his legs Jimmy Sharp stepped off. Coochie couldn't believe how respected Darlene was. During that one night, she learned a whole lot about her new mentor. For the next few days, Coochie hung out with Dameka and Danielle, each of them showed her how they put their game down. Danielle showed Coochie how the Speakeasy got money, and how she had a couple of niggas selling weed too.

Dameka blew Coochie's mind when she showed her how much money the weed spot was getting. She also had a couple of kats getting money for her as well. On the fourth day of her stay in Cook City, Coochie made her decision. "I'm down with this shit ya'll." she announced to Darlene and the girls. "Ya'll are some down-ass bitches."

Dameka, Danielle and Renny were even more pleased than Darlene was; they had really started feeling

Coochie.

"You made the right decision girl." Darlene replied. "This will be the biggest move of your life."

Saturday night they all went out to celebrate; Wanda's Bar on Third Street was the spot this time. Darlene's team was in full effect and it was going down. She led the way with the mindset of an Empress. The other four girls played their positions well. Their goal was the next level, and they were definitely on their way there. While they were out at Wanda's that night, they made about $15,000. The strange thing was that a lot of people were asking about quarters, half grams and grams of coke. They knew that Darlene and her crew didn't sell cocaine but they would ask them anyway. A lot of hustlas, pimps, and hoes had started shooting the shit. As the night wore on, Darlene meticulously took mental notes. Coochie and the rest of the gang were having a ball. While they were out on the dance floor doing 'The Shake' Darlene was sitting at their table making plans.

"What's happenin' lil' mamma?" this kat named Banchey asked, as he strolled up behind her. "You look like you ready for me to take you home; I got a nice warm spot in my bed for you." Darlene looked up at the six-foot, dark-skinned, handsome man and responded, "Not tonight, Banchey. I got a lot of other things on my mind."

"If not tonight, then maybe tomorrow night." Banchey laughed, and then walked away. Darlene

Cook City Publishing

hadn't had a man since Phillip died, and she still wasn't ready to have one. Fifteen minutes later, after everybody returned back to the table, Banchey sent them a bottle of Thunderbird on ice.

"Who was the slim fine thang you were dancing wit'?" Darlene asked Coochie.

"That's this nigga' named Jew, he's from the Southside. He tryin' to lay his game down, but I told the fool he better be ready if he plan to enter in these walls." Renny laughed, and gave Coochie a light hit-five.

"These niggas' out here is down for anything," she smirked. "Gusto just told me that he would leave his wife for a night wit' me."

Dameka joked, "If he willin' to do that, what else is his lame ass willin' to do? My kitty cat needs to be licked!" Darlene gave her sister a sharp look.

At 2:00 a.m., after Wanda's Bar had closed, everybody went up to the Speakeasy. Before opening up, all of the girls changed into jeans and T-shirts. While Danielle, Renny, Dameka and Coochie entertained their customers; Darlene stayed upstairs and thought about what she was going to say to the girls. At 5:00 a.m., they let the last person out and closed up shop. After everything had been cleaned up, Darlene called the meeting. With all of the girls seated before her, she began. "Did anybody ask ya'll about some coke last night at Wanda's?"

Danielle spoke first. "About six or seven niggas and bitches were sweatin' me about the shit."

"They was sweatin' me too," Renny added.

"What about you, Dameka?"

"A couple of people did, but not like Renny and them."

With a serious look on her face, Darlene continued. "The streets are gettin' ready for that shit, and I feel that we should give it to 'em."

"Shit, we might as well." Dameka declared.

"Coochie, Mission is just the nigga to get us what we need." Darlene said.

"I'm on top of that Dee, without a second thought." The discussion went on for a little while longer. Before the meeting ended, they all knew what was about to come into play, and they knew what had to be done. Later on that day, Darlene and Coochie talked to Mission and set everything up. The next morning Darlene, Renny and Coochie were back up in New York. Darlene copped five kilos of coke off of Mission at $15,000 a piece. Mission showed them how to cut it, weight it and bag it up. When he was done, they all knew everything there was to know about the coke game.

"If ya'll break this shit down, ya'll be able to make about two hundred thousand a piece off these kilos."

Liking what she was hearing, Darlene was very pleased with her latest investment. When they got back to Cook City, Darlene distributed the instructions. "Dameka, and Danielle, I want ya'll to continue doing what ya'll been

Cook City Publishing

doing. Renny and Coochie, I want ya'll to handle this coke. Each of us has a job to do, and we must focus on just that. Handle ya'll's bizness and everything will fall into place."

When they hit the streets with that coke, it was like an avalanche. Renny hit Base off and told him what the deal was. Coochie was putting her game down in all parts of the city, just like Darlene knew that she would, she even had that nigga, Jew, hustling for her. The whole city was starting to get 'sniffed out'. Whenever Renny and Coochie went up in a spot, they were guaranteed to make a couple of thousand dollars.

The times were changing and Darlene knew that her crew had to change with them. They even opened up a coke spot down the street from the weed spot on Third Street. Even Rick Doggs stepped up his game. He fell through the Speakeasy and holla'd at Danielle.

"This thing is changin' out here, ma, and I'm tryin' to flip some of that snow once I put my game down on the coke side of things, the streets is gonna be in a chokehold."

"You know I don't deal that shit Rick. I'ma give you Renny's number. She gonna hit you off real proper."

"I need that in my life, ma!"

Danielle's job was hustling weed and running the Speakeasy, and she never forgot it.

Dameka and Pharrel had started drifting apart.

Especially after he found out that she was fucking this young kat named Rob from the projects. He used to get mad at her a lot, but he would never put his hands on her. He knew there would be a severe penalty to pay for an offense like that.

One night while Dameka and Pharrel were together, he committed a crime that was punishable by death. Questioning her in a drunken rage, he put his hands on her.

"Oh, you ain't gonna answer me, huh, bitch!"

"I ain't got to tell you shit, nigga! You better go 'head before you get yo' ass in some trouble."

Furious, Pharrel lashed out and smacked Dameka in the face when he caught her going into her pocketbook for her gun.

"You lame-ass muthafucka!" Dameka yelled, as she placed her hand up to her eye. "My family is gonna kill yo' punk ass!"

"Fuck you and yo' family!" Pharrel yelled back as he began to put on his coat. Knocking Dameka to the floor, he kicked her in the stomach, and walked out of the house. Gasping for air, she moaned and crawled over to the couch. When Renny and Coochie saw Dameka's face, they flipped out. "I'ma kill that muthafucka just as soon as I get my hands on him!" Renny threatened, as she furiously paced the floor.

"Not if I get my hands on him first," Coochie shouted. Renny and Coochie rode around until about a quarter to five the next morning before they spotted

BY THE O.G. WISEMAN

Cook City Publishing

Pharrel selling some weed to one of his customers.

"Wait until them people leave before you pull up on him." Renny instructed Coochie. "I'ma get out and walk around the block so that I can catch him from the blindside."

"Handle ya' bizness, girl." Coochie replied. After the customers pulled off, Pharrel was standing next to his car. Coochie pulled up on him and hollered "You know you gonna pay for that bullshit you did to Dameka, don't you, muthafucka?!"

Caught completely off guard, Pharrel fumbled for the pistol stuck in his waistband. Before he could pull it, Renny crept up behind him. "TOO LATE, BITCH!" she screamed as she shot him in the leg with the 12-gauge shotgun. The single blast almost severed his limb. Falling to the ground, he began to beg. "Come on, ya'll know I would never really hurt Dameka. She's my baby." Coochie got out of the car and whacked him with a 2 by 4 that she carried around in her backseat. "Shut the fuck up! Get yo' bitch ass up and get in the car!"

Coochie and Renny put Pharrel in the backseat of his car and drove him to the train tracks on Seventh Street. When they got there, they wrapped jumper cables around his neck, and hoisted him up on a wire above the tracks. The train yard was dark and silent as a rave. The only sounds to be heard were the scurrying feet of field mice and stray cats. After making sure that Pharrel was up on the wire securely, Renny and Coochie revealed their guns. Gasping and choking, Pharrel's eyes looked as if they were going to pop out of their sockets. Suddenly, red lights started flashing. Just as the sound of the horn from the train went off, Coochie and Renny riddled Pharrel's body with bulletholes BOOM! BOOM! BOOM! BANG! BANG! BOOM! BOOM! BANG! BANG! BANG! BOOM! harrel's body swayed back and forth, jerking and jumping from the force of the relentless blows, as he was used for target practice. The final shot came from Renny. BOOM! She caught Pharrel dead in the forehead, his whole face exploded. "I bet yo' punk-ass won't hit Dameka no mo'" Coochie spat as she and Renny turned and ran back to Pharrel's car.

*　　　　*　　　　*

JUNIOR WAS BECOMING his own man. His mother didn't know it, but he had started selling weed too. He was almost 15 years old, and he was doing things the average kid his age would never dream of. Junior was selling reefer to everybody who smoked it in his school. He even sold reefer to the older kats at the high school. During their lunch breaks, he would flirt with a lot of the girls. At a young age, Junior's game was strong. He may have been younger than the girls, but once he got them in the bed, they thought he was much older than he said he was. Junior was real with all of the things that

Cook City Publishing

he did. In every sense, he was a younger version of his late father.

Christmas of '79 was good one for the whole family. Darlene bought Dameka and Danielle matching burgundy Fleetwood Broughams, with their initials etched in the seat. She copped Coochie and Renny twin caramel colored El Doradoes. For herself, she added a cream colored Sedan Deville to her collection. They were ending the year the way they had lived it, and they were going to bring in the '80's in style.

"We gonna have a crazy New Year's bash down in the Speakeasy." Darlene announced. "Ya'll get ready, cause it's definitely goin' down!"

When New Year's arrived, the Speakeasy was swole. Everybody had on party hats and different colored party masks. Corey was at the door letting the crowd in, and Base was at the bar serving the drinks. All of the playas and pimps had on their best outfits. Wasn't nobody going to be outdone. Darlene, Dameka, Renny, Danielle and Coochie made a grand entrance. Their whole click had on tight leather jumpsuits with matching boots. Darlene's was yellow, Dameka's was powder blue, Danielle's was navy blue, Renny's was red and Coochie's was hot pink. Bad bitches couldn't begin to describe these five. With all eyes on them, Coochie grabbed the microphone. "All ya'll badass hoes and all ya'll muthafuckin' pimps and playas, give it up for my family!" The crowd went wild. Everybody started cheering and making noises with their noisemakers. After Coochie were done, Danielle, Renny and Dameka each said something. The last one to speak was Darlene. "When the clock strikes twelve, I want all of you muthafucka's to say 'get that money in the eighties, baby!'" Then she began the countdown, "Ten! Nine! Eight! Seven! Six! Five! Four! Three! Two! One!"

At the exact stroke of midnight, the whole Speakeasy in a single voice roared, "GET THAT MONEY IN THE EIGHTIES, BABY! HAPPY NEW YEAR!"

The party at the Speakeasy was just what Cook City needed to bring in the New Year. Upstairs, on the third floor of the house, as the clock struck 12, Junior was banging one of Base's hoes' brains out. As he heard everybody downstairs yell, "HAPPY NEW YEAR!" He rolled over and smiled, thinking about the days to come.

CHAPTER FIVE

REMINISCE

PHILLIP HAD been on Darlene's mind a lot lately. It seemed as if every song that she heard reminded her of him. Especially the Commodores. The feeling that she got from the blowing trumpets sent chills through her body and brought tears to her eyes. She had never really mourned his death, so she was feeling it now. Everything else was going good for her and her team. The coke business was doing better than she ever imagined it would. Renny and Coochie were moving keys of coke like they were pounds of weed. Dameka and Danielle were still flooding the streets with that 'Mexican Red-Bud' reefer and the speakeasy was still doing its part. Whenever Darlene sat down to count her money, she would always see Phillip's face. The way that he would smile at her and tell her he loved her.

Lionel Richie had Phillip snapping his fingers and tapping his feet. The whole bar at Wadstacks was right in-sync with him. From one end of the smoke filled room to the other, playas' pimps and some of the baddest broads in the city were two stepping and doing their thing. The small crowd was so alive that it felt like a holiday bash. Done up in a vanilla colored Christian Dior three piece suit, vanilla velour hat, gold specs, and a pair of soft, vanilla colored "crocs", Phillip graced the joint with his undeniable glow. Sitting across from him with a vanilla colored ruffled mini-skirt, and matching high-heeled patent leather knee length boots, Darlene intensified his shine. Feeling the groove all through his body, Phillip couldn't resist any longer. Grabbing Darlene by the hand, without saying a word, he pulled her out onto the dance floor. Two stepping and sliding back and forth, Phillip moved with the type of grace that only a true gangsta could muster. The way that he shook his shoulders and bopped his head was something new.

Darlene bounced and slid along with him. Looking into Phillip's eyes, Darlene could tell how much he loved the song. Knowing that he had a passion for it made her feel it all the more. As the record began to wind down and fade out, Phillip grabbed Darlene's hand again, broke into a step and strolled back over to their table. As soon as they had sat down, the barmaid arrived at their booth with two tall glasses of ripple on the rocks.

"Thank you, Sweetie." Phillip said, handing her a ten dollar bill, "keep the change."

"Thank you." she smiled, stuffing the money in

Cook City Publishing

Cook City Publishing

her bra. Seconds after the short, big-breasted barmaid had walked off, Darlene inquired, "You really like that song, huh baby?"

"Do I? That's one of my favorites." Phillip grinned, "every time I hear that piece, it does something to me."

"Why?"

"You gotta listen to the words, Dee! That nigga Lionel Richie be layin' it down real smooth. I feel everything he's sayin'."

"Oh, yeah?"

"Yeah! Next time you hear that joint make sure that you listen to the words very carefully. I know that nigga is gonna make you feel the same way I do." Phillip couldn't have been more correct. Darlene and Phillip were truly one.

*   *   *

AFTER THE disposal of Pharrel, Dameka drafted a couple more players to her team of hustlas. She opened up spots on both ends of the projects. This short redhead kat named Pooh ran the spot up at the top of the hill, and his gold-toothed homeboy Pee-Wee, ran the one down at the bottom. The projects made about thirty G's a week. Dameka had added two more young studs to the roster and neither of them could keep up with her in bed. She molded them into just what she needed. Renny was getting more money than she could count. The coke spot they had opened up was like a factory. So much paper was coming through that she hired one of Rick Doggs homeboys to hold the door down for her. Malik was gun, and he would spark anything that didn't move right. He was from North Philly, but grew up on the streets of Cook City. Renny would get out of the shower and walk around the spot naked in front of Malik, but she would never allow him touch her.

"If you act right, one day I will give you a shot at the title, until then, be cool, baby."
Renny knew exactly what she was doing. As she kept Malik on his toes, he just waited for his chance to become champ. Danielle was stepping her game up too. She had more, hustlas, gangstas, playas, and pimps coming to the Speakeasy than ever. She would cut at least $5,000 a night from the crap table. The weed was moving like water; everytime Danielle looked up, Corey was telling her that he needed some more. Between the Speakeasy and Corey's spot down on Green Street, they sold at least 50 pounds a week.

Rick Doggs had started selling coke too, and Danielle was pleased with how he handled his business. Things had started out slow for him, but they picked up just like he said they would. Rick Doggs was about the paper and the paper alone.

Coochie was raw and uncut. She had become rawer than the coke that she was selling. She ate, slept and dreamed

Cook City Publishing

BY THE O.G. WISEMAN

about money. If a nigga on the streets wasn't talking about a dollar, then to her, he wasn't talking shit.
On occasion, she would give a lucky contestant a shot of ass, and when she did, you can bet that he was worthy.
Dameka and Danielle were definitely true to the game, and Renny was BAD to the bone! Coochie on the other hand, was Cook City's rookie MVP. Darlene was pleased with her choice of making Coochie a part of the team and so was everybody else. In every aspect, she complimented them to the highest degree. Late one night, as Coochie was coming out of the Speakeasy, heading towards her car, she ran into two of Delaware's finest hustlas.
Rags and Riches were opposites, but they were cut from the same cloth. Rags was high yellow complected, fairly built, with dark eyes and a sandy color, perfectly shaped, afro. Riches was darker than night with a pudgy build, with big eyes and a bald head that shined like a new pair of patent leather shoes. Both of them had mouths full of gold.
    "What's poppin' lil' mamma?" Rags asked as he opened his grey suit jacket, and leaned back with his hand on his hip. Riches chimed in, "You tryin' to have a good time wit' boss playas tonight or what?"
Coochie almost reacted too quickly by reaching into her purse and letting her snub-nosed chrome .357 answer their question. But, just as quickly as she thought about shooting them, she decided to put the two lames to

work for her.

"What ya'll hustlas tryin' to do? I ain't wit' no ménage a trois, but I will definitely give both of ya'll a shot of this pussy. If ya'll can handle it."

"You ain't said nothin' but a word, sugar." Rags responded, rubbing the top of his head.

"We all gonna have some fun tonight." Riches added. "It ain't no fun if my homies can't have none!" Ten minutes later, they were down at the hotel on Reilly Street. Stepping out of the shower, Coochie was asshole naked, dripping wet with water. Her unblemished body was more than a sight to see. Her light brown nipples were hard and pretty. The pubic hairs from her pussy looked fiery, like a burning bush.

"Which one of ya'll is first?" she asked as she rubbed her hands all over her hips in a sensual way. "It's enough for both of ya'll" she smiled sexily. Looking at the lean piece of ass standing in front of him, Rags couldn't help himself. "Let me see if I can make that pussy pop." he answered as he began to undress.

After Coochie got done fucking and sucking Rags, he was worn out, drained and overwhelmed. He rolled over and went straight to sleep. "It's yo' turn now, playa." Coochie purred. Riches was no better than Rags was, his performance was a sequel to what had just happened to his homeboy, only his didn't last half as long. Laughing, Coochie said, "I thought you two niggas were playas. Ya'll can't even handle an uncut

Cook City Publishing

Cook City Publishing

piece of pussy. Now we gonna play by my rules."
Before Rags and Riches left the hotel room the next
morning, they were Coochie's own personal sex toys.
They were ready to do anything for her, even hustle
coke.

*   *   *

"MAN THAT muthafuckin' nigga Rabbit must
think we playin' about that money!" Pee-Wee looked
over at Pooh, spinning the revolver of his .38 special.

"He must not realize he playin' with his life!"

"You know where that nigga's at right now," Pooh
replied nonchalantly.

"Yeah, he should be at his brother's funeral right
now. Joyce told me they was, supposed to be burying
him today."

"Where at?"

"You know Winfield got his hands in that."

"He gonna have his hands in something else if
that nigga Rabbit ain't got that muthafuckin' money
when we see him!" Pee-Wee grinned taking a deep
breath, Pooh raised up from the couch that he had been
sitting on, "Give me a couple of minutes to make sure I
got everything I'ma need, Shit could get real ugly."
Fifteen minutes later, Pooh and Pee-Wee were watching
the small gathering at Howard Day Cemetery as the
minister said his final words over the closed casket that

was already prepared to be lowered into the six-foot grave.

"There that nigga go, right their in the flimsy ass dark black suit," Pee-Wee pointed, feeling himself getting mad.

"Good." Pooh responded. "As soon as the crowd begins to disperse, we gotta go holla at that chump! Come on!" Just as Pooh and Pee-Wee reached the back of the gathering, everyone started walking in different directions. Feeling a light tap on his shoulder, Rabbit turned around. "Hey, what's up ya'll?" he said with a startled look on his face.

"Let me holla at you," Pee Wee placed his finger up to his mouth in a hush tone. "Come on, let's go for a walk!"

Glancing over at Pooh, Rabbit knew it wouldn't be a good idea to resist. Without saying a word, he followed Pee-Wee and Pooh followed him. They walked in the other direction, away from the funeral gathering and towards the woods. Almost 1,000 yards down a grassysloped hill Pee-Wee began,

"What's up wit' that paper you owe us, nigga?" Feeling his head beginning to spin, Rabbit tried to avoid the question. "Man, I'm at my brother's funeral! You think this shit can wait?"

"Wait, Nigga? We done waited long enough for that fifty five hundred; you owe us for that shit. Time to make it right." Pooh frowned. Realizing that he had said the wrong thing, Rabbit tried to go another route,

Cook City Publishing

BY THE O.G. WISEMAN

"Come on baby, me and my family down here is mourning the loss of my brother. At least let me finish that!"

Pee-Wee pulled out his revolver and stuck it in Rabbit's side, "Yo muthafucka, your family is gettin' ready to be mournin' yo' ass too, if you ain't ready to make that count right, lil' Daddy!"

Noticing that Rabbit was desperate and might try to make a break for it, Pooh pulled out a small black jack from the inside of his coat pocket, and smacked him in the back of the head. Falling to the ground unconsciously, Rabbit laid in the grass ready to make his starring debut at his own funeral. Dressed for the part, he was set and ready to go.

"Hurry up! Grab this nigga's legs and let's drag him into the woods," Pooh sneered.

Quickly, the two men carried the act out. Ten feet into the wooded area, they released him. After rummaging through rabbit's pockets, Pee-Wee found $3,200.

"You short, muthafucka." He kicked the unconscious man in the side and woke him up. When Rabbit looked up, he knew that he was on his way to the other side. Pointing his chrome .357 long in Rabbit's face, Pooh laughed. "I'm sorry we ain't got no flowers for yo' petty ass, but that money you still in the red for should get you some real nice black ones in hell! Hopefully you don't owe anybody down there nothin'."

BOOM!

Scurrying through the woods and out the other end of

the cemetery, Pooh and Pee-Wee paid their last respects
to Rabbit.

*   *   *

DARLENE WAS always thinking of new ways to
make money, that was her job. She was head of the
team and if the head couldn't think, then the rest of the
body couldn't operate properly. Darlene always laid
out her plans very carefully. Phillip always told her that
if she didn't think a plan the whole way through, she
would inevitably make careless mistakes. Darlene was
thinking about buying a couple of businesses, but she
couldn't quite decide. After much thought, and a lot of
planning, she came up with the answer. Renny, Danielle,
Dameka and Coochie had become closer than family.
Whenever they did something for themselves, they did
it for everybody. It was one for all, and all for one. If
one of them was hurting, then they all felt pain. If one
of them was happy, then they all shared the joy. If the
sun shined on one of them, then they all got light. They
were the embodiment of 'Am I my sister's keeper'!
On a regular basis, Darlene had started running into
Banchey; he was popping up in the most unexpected
places. She wondered if it was a coincidence, or if he
was planning it that way. He would even pop up behind
her in traffic, blowing and waving at her. When she ran
into him at the corner store on Sixth and Kelker Streets,

Cook City Publishing

Cook City Publishing

she decided to see what was up with him.

"What the deal wit' you, nigga? It seems like everywhere I go, I see you. Are you stalkin' me, or what?" Banchey smiled.

"Be easy, sugar. On the real, I just been tryin' to get wit' you. Everytime I try to holla at you, you give a nigga the brush-off. I know I ain't no ugly nigga, so what's really goin' down? Please let me know the deal, baby girl!"

Darlene looked Banchey in the eye and said, "I ain't really tryin' to get involved with no one right now."

"You ain't had no lovin' since Phillip got killed, Dee. It's about time to get that thing kissed a little bit." Darlene sighed, "Nigga, you crazy."

"Let me take you out to dinner one time. If you ain't feelin' my vibes, I will fade away."

"Alright," Darlene agreed. "After that, you better not be following me around no more or I won't be able to stop somethin' bad from happenin' to you."

That evening Banchey picked Darlene up and took her out to eat at the Ponderosa Steak House. She didn't know why she agreed to have dinner with him, but she did, and she felt anxious to find out the outcome. After a nice dinner, Banchey and Darlene were laughing and talking. When Banchey tried to put his arm around her, Darlene put him in his place.

"Look, playa, I said that I would have dinner wit' you, I didn't say nothin' about fuckin' you. I think that it's time for you to take me home."

"What the deal, Dee?" Banchey asked with a look of confusion on his face.

"You gettin' ready to play ya'self, that's the deal. Now take me home, nigga!"
The ride back to Darlene's house was a silent one. When they arrived back at her crib, she got out and slammed the car door.

"I'm sorry Dee."
Before Banchey could say another word, Darlene walked into the house and closed the door behind her.

*   *   *

JUST AS THE SCHOOL YEAR was ending, one of Junior's old friends came home from Glen Mills Juvenile Placement Center. He had been there for the last two and a half years, locked up for armed robbery. At 16 years old Fro was every bit of 6'5, 215 pounds. He was a mean looking kid with demonic eyes a devilish grin and just like Junior, he looked older than he really was. When Junior first saw Fro, he couldn't stop smiling, no matter how hard he tried.

"What's up lil' nigga?" Junior said jokingly as he gave Fro five, on the backhand side. "It ain't shit," Fro responded with a deep baritone voice.

"I know you glad to be outta that muthafucka. You been away for a nice minute."

Cook City Publishing

Cook City Publishing

"It's all good. A nigga is definitely happy to be back out on the streets."

"Yo, I got some wine and reefer," Junior announced. "I know you tryin' to get high."

"You know I am!" Fro responded with his devilish grin. Junior and Fro went out back in the field where they used to play football and climb trees, and get high. All that day they talked about all the things that had happened since Fro had been locked up and what was going on now. Junior even showed Fro his .22 pistol. Excited and mesmerized, Fro grabbed the gun. "Man, I gotta get me one of these muthafucka's."

"For what, nigga? So you can get yo' fool ass locked back up? It ain't about robbin' and stealin' no mo' playa. It's about gettin' ya hustle on." Junior pulled out a big sack full of nickel bags of weed from the inside of his gray Pony sweatpants.

"This is how I get mines, homey. Since you my nigga, I'ma put you down. You better not fuck up either. I can't afford fuckups. What time you gotta be in the house, nigga?" Junior laughed.

"I go in the muthafuckin' house when I'm ready to!"

"Good, I bet yo' scared ass ain't had no pussy yet. You was only twelve or thirteen when you got locked up."

Fro knew that he had never had any pussy, and he knew that Junior knew it.

"So what, nigga."

"Come on playa, I'ma get you ya first piece of ass. You better be ready."

Fro and Junior walked down on Third Streets where the 'hoe-stroll' was. A badass red-boned chick in black highheeled boots, a white see-through halter top that exposed her breasts, and a tight black miniskirt walked up to Junior and kissed him on the cheek, Fro looked on in amazement.

"Lisa, this is my homeboy Fro, he just came home. He ain't never had no pussy, so I need you to expose him to one of the finer things in life."

"You know I don't be doing this shit for free, but since it's for you, I'ma break the rules."

Junior squeezed Lisa's ass and winked at her. "Follow me baby," Lisa said as she looked over at Fro.

Lisa and Fro walked across the street and entered a brickstoned three story building. Fro was nervous, and shaking like Don Knotts. Upstairs in the second floor bedroom, Lisa didn't waste any time.

"Sit down over there on the bed, sugar," she said as she began to undress. "I'ma take real good care of you, Daddy." Completely undressed, Lisa stood in front of Fro and started playing with herself. Fro had never seen a pussy before in real life and he didn't know what to do or say, he was completely tongue-tied.

"Lay back and relax baby, I'ma make sure that when you get with a woman, you know exactly how to please her."

Going through the motions, Lisa gave Fro his first

Cook City Publishing

blowjob, she sucked his dick so good that he wanted to cry. Then she gave him his first piece of pussy and directed him through all the steps, she even let him slap her on the ass.

"This is my favorite, sugar, it gives me a different type of sensation," she moaned as Fro eased up inside of her. The showstopper was when Lisa taught Fro how to eat pussy; she turned him All-Pro. An hour later, when Fro came back outside, he acted like a totally different person.

When he got back across the street to the steps that Junior was sitting on, there was something different about his face. Looking up at Fro, Junior burst out laughing, "Nigga, wipe that white shit out from around yo' mouth!"

*   *   *

DANIELLE HAD A BIG card game going down in the Speakeasy. Bo, Country and Doe were playing 'Georgia skin'. When the game first started, there were about ten people playing. Four hours later, at 7:00a.m. in the morning, there were just those three players left.

"Nigga, bet ya' pocket on the clean card," Bo yelled. "I got the damn deuce!"

"Bet it, nigga," Doe responded as he spread his bankroll of ten, twenty and hundred dollar bills on the table. Four flips later, Bo's deuce came up. "Pay the Piper, Lame!" Doe shouted, as he laughed, and almost coughed himself into convulsions. Bo was damn near

Cook City Publishing

broke; it took almost all of the money that he had to cover the bet. Now Doe turned his focus to Country. Going back and forth for a couple of hands, they didn't even notice Renny slide up to the table. She pulled out a nice size stack of hundred dollar bills, and sat them down in front of her. Bo peeped at the money stack and went right for it.

"My ten is the baddest muthafucka in the deck! Anybody say it ain't, get ya' weight up!"
Looking down at her queen, Renny responded, "I ain't tryin' to be here all morning. Let it all ride on this badass bitch!"
Doe had the ace, and Country had the ten, flipping the next card, Danielle turned Country's ten over. "Damn!" Country said with a look of disbelief and disappointment on his face. Renny and Doe disregarded him and focused on the next card. "Hold up, Danielle," Doe protested before she flipped the next one. Pulling out the keys to his Mark V Lincoln, Doe continued, "Bet these too, sugar!"

"You ain't said nothin' but a word daddy." Renny retorted, pulling out the keys to her car, and slamming them on the table. Country and Bo's eyebrows rose.

"Turn them muthafucka's out," Renny insisted. Danielle took the cards out of the box and turned them over. Doe's ace was the second one from the top, his mouth opened and his head dropped. Renny smiled. "Somebody gotta lose, and somebody gotta win." She raked the money up, dropped the keys to the Mark V

BY THE O.G. WISEMAN

Cook City Publishing

Lincoln in her pocketbook, and then turned to Doe. Peeling off one of the hundred dollar bills, she slid the stack over to him. "I like ya' style playa, but don't ever bet against me. Go get ya' weight back up, and then get my money back to me."

Darlene's heart had been feeling rather heavy ever since her date with Banchey. She couldn't get Phillip off of her mind. Waking up the next morning, Darlene bought a dozen red roses and rode up to Phillip's gravesite. Sitting down beside his tombstone, she began to cry. The sky was a gloomy grey with low hanging overburdened clouds. A strong wind was blowing fallen leaves swiftly across the graveyard and around her. Darlene missed Phillip so much. No matter how much money she had, it would never be able to fill the void that his death had left in her life. As Darlene sat there wiping the tears from the corners of her eyes, she began to reminisce about the good times that they had together. As the memories came flooding back, so did the tears. And with each tear she wiped away a smile took its place.

Phillip and his cousin Coota walked into the house with an armful of bags and dropped them down in the middle of the living room floor. In the kitchen cooking dinner, Darlene wiped her hands on her apron and hurried to see what type of surprise her husband had for her this time. Turning to Coota, Phillip said, "Make sure you tell Walt and 'em to be ready. You know we gotta ride down to North Carolina in the mornin' to meet James Brown! We gotta catch that nigga before he get all high and drunk out of his damn mind!" Coota chuckled, "I know that's right! That nigga acted a damn fool last time we went to Alabama together."

"Make sure Ben and 'em is ready too. You talk to Owen today?"

"Yeah, I was over his spot early this mornin'." He told me he had to go get some new guitar strings. He should have 'em by now."

"Cool, Daddy-O. Make sure you check and recheck everything before you start partyin' tonight! You need a couple of dollars?"

"Nah, I'm straight baby. Once I go over there and get what T.J. owes us, I should definitely be straight."

Coota and a few of his homeboys had a little in-house band that often opened up for James Brown and a couple other up-and-coming kats. 'The Cook City Crooners', they were just that. The lead singer, Walter Jiggs would often sing broads right out of their panties. When Coota got on stage and started sliding around, doing splits and screaming, a lot of the chicks had to be tended to, placing cold rags on their foreheads they were taken out to the lobby. Sometimes, they would even have to be taken to the hospital and when 'The Crooners' opened up for the 'Godfather', everybody knew that it was going to be a show to remember.

"Alright, Playa," Phillip patted Coota on the

Cook City Publishing

𝕮𝖔𝖔𝖐 𝕮𝖎𝖙𝖞 𝕻𝖚𝖇𝖑𝖎𝖘𝖍𝖎𝖓𝖌

back, *"Make sure that everybody is straight and meet me down at Otto's at 11:00p.m. tonight."*

Turning to greet his queen, Phillip walked over to Darlene, and kissed her passionately on the lips. "Hey sweet mamma," he smiled. "You taste like you been in that honey again." Darlene blushed, "Now what is all the stuff in these bags, Phillip?"

"You know I bought my baby nothin' less than what she deserves, all of this is for you!" Looking down at what was at least six shopping bags and a coat-box from 'Macs', Darlene shook her head, "I don't know what I'm gonna do wit' you."

"I do." Phillip smiled shyly.

Picking up the coatbox first, Darlene opened it up and almost fainted at the sight of the mink shawl. "How did you know I wanted one of these?"

"That's my job, baby!"

Trying it on, Darlene pictured herself stepping out of the Cadillac with it draping from her shoulders. Opening up the rest of the gifts, she was amazed more and more by Phillip's knowledge of some of her heart's deepest desires. Caught up in the moment, forgetting about the food cooking on the stove, Phillip and Darlene intertwined on the couch and engaged in an act that took them both to ecstasy.

Darlene knew that if Phillip were watching, he wouldn't be very proud of her, at that moment. She knew that he would want her to carry on; he wouldn't accept any of her crying. Darlene knew that if she allowed herself to become weak, her whole foundation was liable to crumble right up under her feet. She had to take care of Junior and the four girls that she knew depended on her for guidance and direction. Pulling herself together, Darlene got up, dusted herself off, and looked up to the sky. She knew that if she kept making the right decisions, everything would be all right.

Before leaving Phillip's gravesite Darlene spoke to him, "I love you baby, and I always will. The tears that I shed are not from weakness, but because I miss you so much." Turning to leave, Darlene heard Phillip's voice, *"It's okay, baby girl. I know how much you love me. Hold ya' head and do what you think is best for you and Junior. Don't ever forget that whoever controls the money controls the streets."*

Then like a sudden summer breeze, the voice was gone.

Cook City Publishing

CHAPTER SIX

MORE PROBLEMS

DARLENE AND HER squad was milkin' the streets
for every dollar that they could. If there was a dollar
to be made, they made it. After ten months of straight
hustlin', Darlene went out and bought a baby mansion
on the outskirts of Cook City. It was a beautiful home
with seven spacious bedrooms; five bathrooms, two
kitchens, a private office in the basement and a balcony
that encircled the entire top part of the house. It had
three two-car garages and a small pond out back.
Entering the front gates, it had a horseshoe driveway
with two marble pillars at the entrance. The two acres
of land that the house sat on were filled with cherry and
apple trees; the set-up was something straight out of
the 'Lifestyles of the Rich and Famous'. When Darlene
brought the girls out to see their new home, they
couldn't believe it was theirs. "Damn, girl, you sure this

place is big enough for all of us?" Renny joked as she looked around at the baby mansion.

"I know this ain't our house!" Dameka screamed in amazement. "Only movie stars live like this!" Darlene took the girls on a tour of the whole house and when she showed them their bedrooms, they almost fainted. Renny ran to her bed like a big kid and jumped on it. The bed was so soft that she didn't even bounce, managing to crawl out of the queen-sized cushion, she walked around and admired all of the pretty furniture that decorated the room.

"Girl, this place is like a dream come true. When we were little, I always dreamed of having a room like this!"

Amazed by the size of the bathroom inside her bedroom, Danielle sat down on the side of round porcelain bathtub, and rubbed her hand across the brass dolphins that were mantled at each end. "Ten people can fit in this muthafucka, it's almost as big as a swimming pool!" she laughed. Dameka and Coochie were also thrilled with their new dwellings. Darlene had decorated everything just to their liking. The last thing that Darlene showed the girls was the home-office located right beneath the kitchen. In the middle of the room sat a big round meeting table with five chairs placed around it. In the far-left corner was a 50-gallon fish tank populated by baby sharks. At the rear of the room was Darlene's own personal handcrafted mahogany desk, with a door centered directly behind it.

Cook City Publishing

A poster-sized painting of Phillip graced the right half of the wall. The portrait was a perfect likeness of him. The office was cozy and quaint, and it brought all of the girls a feeling of security.

"This is where we will have all of our meetings. We gonna keep the other house, but this is where we will live. Whatever is done in the streets stays in the streets, we can't allow anyone to enter our world." Looking around the room at each of the girls, Darlene continued, "I love all of ya'll bitches, and don't ya'll every forget that! It's not about me, and it's not about you. It's about us."

Teary eyed, Coochie walked up to Darlene and hugged her. "We love you to Dee."

*   *   *

JUNIOR HAD Lisa open for business; she would do anything for him. Even sell pussy, if he ever asked her to. Just as Lisa placed her arm around Junior's neck and kissed him on the cheek, Base turned the corner at Third and Reilly Streets. Furious at what he was witnessing, Base pulled his aqua colored Cadillac over and jumped out. "Bitch, I know you ain't givin' my pussy away for free!" Startled, Lisa quickly backed away from Junior and lowered her head to the ground.

"Get yo' muthafuckin' ass over here and get in the car, and hurry the fuck up!"

As Lisa walked past Base to get into the car, he slapped the shit out of her. Lisa stumbled a couple of feet and then regained her balance. Base had never seen Junior before, so he didn't know that the young kat standing before him was related to Renny.

"Young nigga, what the fuck you think this is? If you don't break yo'self, I'ma put yo' young ass in ya place!"

Junior tensed up, ready to snap. "Listen here lame, if you can't control yo' hoes, then I guess somebody else will have to do it, don't get mad 'cause one of yo' bitches chose me."

Insulted by Junior's words, Base backhanded him, busting his lip, blood ran down the side of Junior's mouth. Before Junior could react, Base had his .38 revolver in his face.

"Now, break yo'self young nigga, before I be sendin' yo' mamma flowers." Shocked and enraged Junior turned, and ran down the street. BOOM! BOOM! BOOM! BOOM! Base fired in the air. "If I catch yo' young ass down here again, I'ma let you feel some of this heat!"

Lisa was sitting in Base's car scared to death. She knew that he was going to punish her for breaking the rules. A couple of hours later, Junior caught up with Fro.

"Yo, remember that chick Lisa that hit you off when you first came home?"

"Yeah," Fro answered.

"Well, I was just down on the 'hoe-stroll' chillin'

Cook City Publishing

wit' that bitch, when her lame ass pimp rolled up on us."

Taking a good look at Junior; Fro noticed that his lip was swollen. He became outraged. "What the fuck happened!

"That nigga got the drop on me, and pulled his pistol!"

"I'ma kill that nigga!" Fro roared as he began to pace back and forth. Junior thought that Fro was joking around, but only because he didn't know how serious Fro was. Around 1:00 a.m. that night, Fro was hanging down on Third Street, he was drunk as a muthafucka, looking for Base. Taking the last drag from his cigarette, he threw it to the ground and stomped it out. At that very moment Base pulled up on Third and Calder Streets and started talking to one of his hoes. As Base was tongue-lashing her, Fro walked up to the driver's side window. Base and the broad both looked up, wondering what was going down. Annoyed by the interruption, Base almost lost his cool. What it be like, young nigga? You lookin' for a nice piece of trim or what?"

Fro stared at Base with fire in his eyes, and pulled his nickel-plated .22. BOOM! BOOM! BOOM! BOOM! BOOM! BOOM! Six shots to the head left Base brainless, with chunks of meat and blood splattered all over his car. The broad that Base was with dropped to her knees, and placed her hands in front of her face. Fro placed his gun back in the holster and staggered to the left a little bit.

"That's what it be like, you hoe-ass pimp!"

*　　　　　*　　　　　*

THE SOUND of Isaac Hayes filled the air as Darlene, Danielle, Dameka, Renny, and Coochie came stepping through the door. All of the girls were dressed down in Jordache jean suits, except for Darlene. She had on a Jordache jean skirt-suit. All of them had on black six-inch suede cowgirl boots, with gold tips on the front of them. Darlene's had gold tassels. Diamond necklaces, rings and bracelets that they had on, lit up the place. Lou spotted them and told the bartender to give them whatever they asked for, on the house. Seated at the table in the back of the bar, Lou came over and greeted them. "Sugar, sugar, sugar, damn! Ya'll lookin' fine tonight! A nigga might pay a pretty penny to hang out wit' ya'll."

"Slow down, low down," Renny said, rolling her eyes at him. "You can't handle nothin' at this table!" Clowning Lou, Coochie stood up and poked her ass out at him. Everybody laughed. They had love for Lou, but they knew he was a trick-ass nigga. Darlene sneered, "Lou, you know you my main man, how much paper you willin' to give me to be wit' one of these Asiatic queens?"

"I got about forty-five thousand in my pocket, but

before the night is over I should have a couple more thousand," he answered with a devilish grin on his face. When Darlene looked up from her table, Banchey was staring dead in her face. As he tried to wave at her, she quickly looked away. Dick Dastardly staggered over to where the small entourage was seated, with a bottle of Thunderbird in his hand.

"Did ya'll hear about Base? Somebody blew his muthafuckin' head off down on Third Street. The word that I got was that some young nigga sent him on his way."

Jarred by the news, Renny's eyebrows crinkled. Quickly, she dismissed her thoughts. If Base was gone, then she would just have to replace him. Dameka had the giggles all night. Every time somebody said something to her, she would bust out laughing. Coochie had her eye on this playa named B.J. from Rochester, New York. He had just arrived in town and everybody was talking about him. Just looking at B.J. turned Coochie on, and she knew that he was going to be hers. Danielle was thinking about Rick Doggs. '*When I get home, I need him to scratch this itch I got*,' she thought to herself. The whole squad was having fun, and that really pleased Darlene. They were living life the way it was supposed to be lived, they were doing it big. Each day, the hustle was growing. And with more money came more problems, so much money was being made that Darlene was anticipating something crazy. Before those thoughts were completely out of her mind, something crazy did

Cook City Publishing

happen. Dameka rode down to York, Pennsylvania to drop off five pounds of weed to this young kat name Hootie. While she was gone, Corey broke into the weed spot down on Third Street, and stole twenty-five pounds, he would have gotten away with it if Dick Dastardly hadn't seen him. Dameka had paid Dick Dastardly to watch the spot while she was gone and when she got back, he told her exactly what happened. Dameka was furious but she knew she had to handle the situation the right way. Renny and Coochie came up with the perfect plan to set Corey's no good, lame ass up. Never letting on that she knew what had happened, Dameka called Corey around 11:00 p.m. that night.

"What's up playa?" she said, when he answered the phone.

Trying to play it cool, Corey responded in a smooth tone, "It ain't shit baby girl, just sittin' here thinkin' about bumpin' and grindin' wit' you."

Dameka winced, biting her tongue. "Me and you must be on the same page. I was just thinking about the same thing."

"What?"

"Yeah! Me, Renny and Coochie are having a party, and I thought specifically about you."

"Oh yeah! What type of party?"

"You know, just us four doing whatever comes natural."

Corey paused for a moment, not wanting to seem anxious, then the thought of fucking all three of them

Cook City Publishing

fine ass bitches popped into his mind, he couldn't resist. At 12:30 a.m., Corey arrived down at the Sunrise Inn on Front Street. Dameka answered the door asshole naked, looking finer than Kelley Lanette Allen. Corey's mouth started watering. As he stepped through the door he noticed that Renny and Coochie were dressed in the same attire. Eyeing the place-full of pussy, he immediately got an erection.

"Shit nigga, you might as well take off your clothes too," Renny insisted; laying on the bed with her legs wide open. Without any hesitation, Cory began to undress. Dameka was looking at him the whole time, wanting to put a bullet in his head right then and there. Coochie got up from the bed where she was sitting sashayed past him into the bedroom. Switching her big, thick fine hips with each step, as soon as Corey was done undressing, Coochie came back with two .44 magnums in her hands.

"I knew you didn't think you was gonna get away wit' robbin' our spot, did you? You lame ass trick!" Shocked, Corey tried to speak, "I...I...I..." he stammered. Renny got up and pimp-slapped the taste outta his mouth! "Lyin' is only gonna make matters worse for you, nigga!"

While Coochie held Corey at gunpoint, all of the girls got dressed. After they were dressed, Renny tied his hands behind his back. As Corey tried to speak again, Dameka kicked him in the face. The force from the kick knocked a couple of his teeth out, pushing him forward

Cook City Publishing

to the floor. Renny walked outside and made sure that the coast was clear; they walked Corey to the car and told him to get in the trunk.

Inside the cold, dark trunk, Corey began to cry. Five miles up the river, Coochie pulled over into the wooded area and let Corey out. Bing! Dameka blindsided him with a crowbar, sending him straight to the ground. Panic-stricken, Corey laid on the ground with a terrified look on his face, too scared to even speak.

Coochie walked up and stood over him with the twin magnums in her hands. BOOM! Her first shot blew Corey's dick and balls to smithereens.

"AAAHHH!" Corey yelled, as he began to spasm. BOOM! The second slug tore Corey's stomach open, leaving him intestine-free. There was no room for his pleading and crying. Renny stuck the barrel of the gage in Corey's mouth and pulled the trigger BOOM! Dameka smiled, "Bye-bye muthafucka!"

The police downtown were starting to hear Darlene's name a lot. Every time they turned around, somebody was talking about Dee Dennison and her crew. When the white-haired officer with the grimacing face heard Darlene's name, he was furious. "I'm gonna get that bitch, just like I got her husband," he told himself. Ever since the day that Darlene threw his card on her doorstep, he knew that their paths would cross again.

Hearing the news about the termination of Base, Junior knew that Fro was his homeboy for life. Junior wasn't exactly glad that Fro had killed Base, but it sure saved

him the trouble of having to deal with the situation.
On his way down to Third and Herr Streets, Junior ran
into Lisa. She was very excited to see him. "What's up
baby?" she said as she ran up to him. "I haven't seen
you in awhile. I know you heard about what happened
to Base. Yo' smooth ass probably did it! Anyway, you
know I need a new sugar daddy now. You my number
one candidate.
Junior smirked, "Pimpin' ain't my thing, baby girl. I'ma
hustla."

"Don't say I didn't give you a chance. Before you
know it, some lame-ass nigga is gonna be down here
tryin' to call the shots wit' his foot in my ass."

"I'ma holla at you later on, Lisa. I got some
bizness to handle." Before Junior walked away, Lisa
gave him $500. "That ain't shit baby. I'm the best hoe
on the strip. Put me under ya' wing, and watch how
much paper you really see."
For the rest of the day, Junior thought about what Lisa
had said to him, he began to wonder how strong his
pimp game could really be.

*　　　　*　　　　*

AT 6:30 A.M. in the morning, after everybody had
left the Speakeasy, the police kicked in the front door.
Coochie and Danielle heard the commotion upstairs,
and quickly stashed everything. The last thing that

they did was grab the money and their guns. Then, they slipped out through the secret panel. The officer with the grimacing face just missed them as he came storming down the stairs. He searched the whole spot and didn't find a thing.

A few hours later, there was a warrant out for Darlene's arrest. When the police arrived at the house on the outskirts of Cook City, they could only serve her a citation. It wasn't a crime to have beer and liquor in your residence, but it was a crime to sell it without a license. The police couldn't prove that Darlene had done anything wrong, so they were just trying to shake her up. The officer with the grimacing face was sure that somebody had been in that house, but he couldn't prove it.

Danielle and Coochie told Darlene the whole story, she knew that whatever had happened wasn't supposed to have happened and she wanted to make sure that it never did again.

"We gotta figure out who put the police on us. We can't be havin' this type of shit goin' down, it hurts our paper. Until we get to the bottom of this shit, we got a major problem."

Danielle, Dameka, Renny and Coochie all looked at one another. After Darlene was done talking to her team, they all hit the streets to find out what was going on. Somebody knew something, and it was only a matter of time before the information leaked out.

Cook City Publishing

CHAPTER SEVEN

LOVE & LOYALTY

DUTCHIE COBB was standing on the corner of Sixth and Delaware streets looking for his next fix when Dameka pulled up on him. "Dutchie Cobb, let me holla at you for a minute playa."

Pleased to see one of the finest bitches in Cook City, Dutchie Cobb grinned and walked up to the passengers' side window. "What it be like baby doll? You tryin' to get wit' a nigga or what," he joked.

With a serious look on her face, Dameka replied, "You know the police ran up in our Speakeasy. Did you hear anything about who might have put them onto us?"

"Naw, baby doll, I ain't heard shit about that, but if and when I do, you and ya peoples will be the first ones to know."

"You do that Dutchie," Dameka continued, "keep ya ear to the streets for me." Dameka went inside of her pocketbook and handed Dutchie Cobb a $100 bill.

"If you come through with the information that I need I got something else for you too." then she pulled off. Meanwhile, over on the southside of town, Coochie was talking to Fat Patty about what happened.

"Girl, you know if I hear something I'ma tell ya'll," Fat Patty said, as she began breaking the pound of weed down that Coochie had just given her.

"I need you to find out anything you can about this shit!"

"I got you girl."

Frustrated, Coochie got up and walked to the front door. "I got some other bizness to go handle, make sure that you look into that I will holla back at you later on." On her way back uptown, Coochie saw Junior walking down Seventh Street, he was dressed in a grey and white Pierre Cardin velour sweatsuit and a pair of white-on-white Jack Percell sneakers. From behind Coochie almost didn't recognize him, but his uptown hook and stroll gave him away. Coochie pulled up on him, Junior smiled and hopped into the car.

"What's poppin' Cooch," Junior said jokingly, as he reached over and gently kissed her on the cheek. Astonished, Coochie blushed. "Boy, you better stop that! You know you too young for me. This ocean is too deep for you to swim in." Coochie knew that Junior had a crush on her, but it never went any further than that. In her own little way, she dug the young kat too. There was something about him that made her tingle inside. As Coochie pulled away from the curb, she looked over

Cook City Publishing

BY THE O.G. WISEMAN

at Junior and knew that one day she was going to give him some pussy. She just didn't know when that day would come. Riding along in the car they both could feel the electric vibes between them.

"Where you coming from?" Coochie inquired.

"Now, why you wanna know that?" Junior answered back.

"No real reason boy, I was just wondering what you were doin' down here walkin'."

"If you really wanna know, I just came from the projects tearin' some young broads back out the frame." Junior smiled. Coochie looked over at him evasively.

"Boy, you too much!"

"I know that's right," Junior responded.
At Sixth and Dauphin Streets Coochie dropped Junior off. Looking at him and shaking her head, she said, "Boy, you better be good!"

*   *   *

Danielle was in and out of every bar in town, and nobody knew anything. She was really baffled about this one. Somebody always knew something! Nothing went on in the city that she and her family couldn't find out about, money always made people talk. But this time, it didn't seem to be helping.

*   *   *

QUEEN BEE

STROLLING THROUGH the door of the Red Dot
Pool Hall, dressed in a black peacoat, black leather
applejack, some fringed blue jeans, and a pair of black
Stacy Adams boots. Rick Doggs had a crazy look in
his eyes, each pool table was occupied by a couple of
kats shooting eight ball or gambling at nine ball. The
house man, Harry O., was sitting in the rear of the joint,
smoking a cigar, waiting to wrack the balls.

"What's up Rick Doggs?" Harry O. yelled out
over the small portable radio that was playing the Isley
Brothers 'Choosy Lover'.

"What it be like, baby?" Rick Doggs responded,
eyeing all of the occupants in the establishment.
Stopping at the first table, Rick Doggs continued, "Turn
that radio off for a second Harry O.! I got somethin'
that I need to say!" Quickly complying with the young
hustla's request, the houseman killed the music. Looking
around the gloomily lit room, Rick Doggs wanted to
make sure he had everybody's attention before he began.
When he was sure that the time was right, he spoke.
"Now, I ain't sayin' that ya'll did, but in any event that
any of ya'll did, I need to know if you heard about who
put police on my people's Speakeasy?"
Feeling disrespected by the audacity of a nigga that
wasn't even from Cook City, all of the young kats in the
rear, at the last table, started laughing. "Who the fuck is
yo' peoples?" Tevall Thunder asked. "And why the hell
is you up in here askin' us, nigga?"

Cook City Publishing

BY THE O.G. WISEMAN

"I just thought ya'll niggas might point a playa in the right direction."

"The right direction is out that muthafuckin' door, nigga! You comin' up in here like you a private investigator or somethin'!"

Maintaining his composure, Rick Doggs walked to the back of the poolroom where the small crowd of young kats were shooting nine-ball. "You being' real disrespectful, homeboy," Rick Doggs said, addressing the 5'9 and stocky built Tevall.

"Nigga, fuck you!" Tevall shot back. "Who the fuck is you for me to be respectin?"

Standing up, Harry O. went to say something to cut through the tension which was so thick only a hacksaw could have penetrated it. Before he opened his mouth, Rick Doggs slid up on a Tevall, grabbed him by the neck, and was pressing a cold piece of steel up under his chin. "Now, what's that bullshit you was just talkin', fat rat!" Rick Doggs frowned with his finger itching to squeeze the trigger of his .44. "You's a real disrespectful ass nigga! Where I come from, niggas like you get silenced quickly!"

The rest of the young kats standing around the table backed away, hoping that Rick Doggs didn't turn his gun on them after he finished with Tevall. Tevall suddenly got constipation of the mouth.

"What you got to say now, huh, Lil Daddy?" Rick Doggs pressed his .44 harder into Tevall's Adam's apple. "Come on now, baby," Harry O. pleaded, trying to prevent bloodshed in his establishment. "All this ain't necessary."

Hearing the houseman's words brought Rick Doggs back to a state of sanity. Slamming Tevall up against the wall, he slowly backed away. "Ya'll young niggas is in luck! If it wasn't for Harry O., it woulda definitely been some slow singin' up in this bitch tonight!

"The question I asked about my peoples' Speakeasy, forget it! But that's my word, if I find out that any of ya'll had somethin' to do wit' it or even knew about it, we gonna do a lil' slow dancin'!"

Shaking his head back and forth, Rick Doggs glanced at Harry O. and then strolled back out of the poolroom.

*   *   *

RENNY KNEW this young vice cop named Jonesey. If anybody knew what was going on, she was sure that he did. Jonesey would tell Renny anything she wanted to know. But for his valuable piece of information, he would never ask her for money, all he wanted was a stiff shot of ass. Renny didn't mind fucking him, even though he had a little dick, because Jonesey sure could eat pussy good. Jonesey met Renny behind the carwash up on Sixth Street. She was laid back in the seat of her Mark V Lincoln waiting for him with nothing on but a black see-through blouse, knee-highs, and a pair of ankle length boots. Her legs were sprawled wide open.

Cook City Publishing

BY THE O.G. WISEMAN

He looked inside of the car and hopped inside the backseat with her.

"Now, don't this look good?" Renny asked as Jonesey cocked her right leg up. "Come get some baby, if you want it."
Jonesey dove straight in the pussy face first; he was like a fat kid eating Jell-O pudding. A few minutes later he went up inside of her. They had the charcoal colored Lincoln rocking and reeling. During intermission, Jonesey told Renny everything that she wanted to know.

"Yeah, baby girl, you know that junkie-ass nigga named Blue Notes? Well, he's the one that gave us all the information we needed. For whatever reason, this lame-ass nigga don't like ya'll. My suggestion is that ya'll don't let him know nothin', because he's gonna tell it." Renny knew exactly who Blue Notes was, and she knew exactly why he was telling on them. With a look of confusion on her face, Renny spoke, "What the fuck is Blue Notes tellin' on us for? I don't even know that nigga, for real. I may have seen him once or twice."

"Well, that's what it is baby girl."
Throwing Jonesey off further, Renny continued, "I'm glad that you let me know, sugar. I'm gonna have to be on the lookout for him."
With intermission over, Renny gave Jonesey some more pussy, twenty minutes later, Jonesey was gone, Renny got dressed and paid some young kat at the car wash to clean her car.

Cook City Publishing

QUEEN BEE

Darlene wanted to get to the bottom of the situation in a hurry; she knew that if somebody was out there giving up information their whole operation was being jeopardized. Darlene knew she wasn't by herself; she had faith in her squad. *'If there's a problem out there, I know that my girls will take care of it'*, she thought to herself.

After copping a $20 bag of heroin from her homegirl, Weisy, Renny took the bag of dope, mixed it with battery acid and went to handle her business. Blue Notes' lame ass was standing down on Fourth Street in front of the abandoned building where all of the dope addicts hung out. The old house was used as a shooting gallery, and as a haven for crackheads. When Renny pulled up on Blue Notes, his eyes got as wide as silver dollars, and she could tell he was ready to run. "Blue Notes, let me holla at you playa. I ain't on that other shit no more, we gonna let that die." Blue Notes was really apprehensive. "What…what…what…what's up baby girl?" he stammered, as he moved slowly towards the car.

"I need you to help me move some of this 'China White' we just got in."

Blue Notes' whole demeanor changed and instantly he started sweating. "If it's some good shit, you know I can move it."

Renny knew he would take the bait. "Me and my peoples always have the best shit. The streets will tell you that."

"I'm feeling you baby girl, but I just can't go

Cook City Publishing

148

Cook City Publishing

puttin' my name on anything. I need something to test," he said as he looked away from her. Renny had him.

"Here, nigga, here goes a lil' sample. "Be easy with this shit, I know it's the rawest thing on the streets."

When Blue Notes heard that, he wanted to main line the whole bag. "I'ma be back in a lil' while, nigga. Let me know what it's hittin' fo'," then she pulled off.

Bypassing all of his junkie friends and crack addicts on the first and second floors, Blue Notes went straight up to the attic, the room was pitch black. All of the windows were boarded up, the only light in the room came from the tall pole outside, illuminating the cracks and crevices. The only furnishings were two metal milk crates, a pissy-smelling mattress and a worn wooden table, the air in the old house was stale and putrid. Blue Notes wasn't trying to share his bag with anybody, if it was as raw as Renny said that it was, he knew he was going to get the type of high he was looking for. Nervous, jittery and anxious, "Damn, I gotta take a shit," he said out loud. Blue Notes got situated on one of the metal crates and cooked his dope up. Filling the syringe with the cooked up poison, Blue Notes found his vein and hit it. The dope eased into his system, suddenly, he felt a tremendous rush of sweat start gushing from his pores. Twitching and jumping, it became hard for him to breathe; his heart was racing pounding thunderously. With each breath it felt like his heart was going to explode. Blue Notes knew that something was wrong but there was absolutely nothing he could do. Harder and harder his heart violently pounded, as his eyes began to roll back into his head. Blue Notes grabbed his chest as he fell back up against the wall. Gasping for air, with the needle still in his arm Blue Notes tried to call for help, but it was useless. His cries fell on ears as deaf to the world as his, crashing spasmodically against the wall again his chest exploded. As burning urine streamed down his leg, he defecated on himself, and in that moment, his soul ebbed from his lifeless body.

*   *   *

RICK DOGGS was making a lot of moves, he was moving more coke than anybody in the City, except for Renny and Coochie. Rick Doggs was the youngest kat in the game if a person didn't know him, they would never know that he was a hustla. He was real laid back, and he always rolled by himself. Rick Doggs' motto was, *"If I have to kill a nigga, who's gonna tell? I ain't!"*

"Baiter! What it be like, baby?" Rick Doggs greeted the older kat as he slid into the passenger's side of the dark colored Bonneville and shook Baiter's hand. "What's up youngin," the grey haired oldhead responded, flicking his toothpick around in his mouth, "That last package you dropped on me was real proper! I had to get me a hoe and hide out for a couple of days, niggas

Cook City Publishing

Cook City Publishing

was sweatin' me so much!"

"I told you that piece was raw, playa." Rick Doggs smiled, "You must'a ran outta that shit real quick if you hid out for a couple of days!"

"Man that shit went like hotcakes at a pancake jamboree!" They laughed. Looking into the sun-visor mirror, Baiter patted his afro to make sure that it still looked the same way that it did a couple of hours before when he had left 'Porter's Barbershop' on Sixth and Kelker Streets.

"I think I'ma have to double up this time, lil' Daddy."

"You sure you can handle that?" Rick Doggs inquired with a serious look on his face, "A hundred grams is kinda steep!"

"Now all of a sudden you wanna question what I can handle!" Baiter cut his eyes at Rick Doggs, "You must be forgettin' who helped you out when you first came through wit' that package, lil' nigga! If ya oldhead tell you I can handle that, then I got it!"

"I didn't say you couldn't handle it, baby! All I said was it's kinda steep."

"Steep my ass! I make sure you get yours off the rip, don't I?" Before Rick Doggs could answer, Baiter continued, "I make five thousand dollars during the night. Imagine what I can do if I really put my hustle down, young nigga! You ain't talkin' to no slouch! I came up wit' the best of 'em! When a nigga first said, *'If it don't make dollars, it don't make sense'*, he was quoting me!"

Handing Rick Doggs the manila envelope containing
the $5,000 that he owed him on the last package, Baiter
straightened the diamond pinky ring that adorned his
right hand.

"Now what we gonna do, youngin'? I gotta whole
lotta' hustlin to do!"

Sticking the envelope in the inside pocket of his tweed
Calvin Klein blazer, Rick Doggs smiled, "Gimme a half
hour, pimp! Meet me down at the mini-mart on Sixth
and Division Streets. This is a big step for you, oldhead.
Don't step outta bounds! I ain't gotta run the rules to
the game down to ya. You already know that the penalty
is death!"

Without saying another word, Rick Doggs got out of the
car, strolled around the corner and hopped into a pecan
colored Seville with gangsta whitewalls on it.

*   *   *

The Speakeasy had been closed for a couple of weeks
after the joint had been unsuccessfully raided. Darlene
came through to make sure that everything was running
smoothly. She even rode around the block a couple of
times to make sure that she didn't see any unmarked
cars in the area. As Darlene was parking her car down
the street from the spot, Banchey walked up with a
sympathetic look on his face.

"What it be like, brown sugar? I hope you ain't

Cook City Publishing

still mad at me." Annoyed by Banchey's presence, Darlene responded "What you want Banchey? I told you that I didn't want to see you no more."

"Come on baby girl. Don't act like that, I'm sorry if you felt that I disrespected you in any way. I was just tryin' to show you how much I was feelin' you."

"Well, I wasn't feelin' that!"

"Just give me one more chance, I promise not to cross the line. I will do whatever you want me to do." Darlene laughed. "Nigga, you sound like a lame. If you keep that shit up, I definitely ain't gonna fuck wit' you." Darlene and Banchey went back and forth for a few minutes. "I will let you know when I'm ready, until then I need you to give me my space." Hearing Darlene's response, Banchey saw a ray of hope. "I'ma give you that, baby girl, just don't take too long."

   *   *   *

JUNIOR AND Fro stepped up their game too. Even though they weren't getting the type of money that his mother and her crew were getting, they were on top of things.

"Man, I ain't never seen this type of money," Fro said excitedly. "If we keep this shit up we gonna be millionaires before we hit twenty-one!"

"That's the purpose nigga, we in it for the money, and nothing else." Junior and Fro had about $8,000.

Every penny that they made, they flipped, everything got broken down. Off of the eight G's, Junior could see them making $25,000 easily, hustling was in his blood and he knew how to do it very, very well.

"We doin' good but it's time for us to take it to the next level," Junior told Fro. "If we gonna build something, it's gotta be solid."
Junior's mind was always on hustling, but lately he had been thinking about Lisa and the proposal that she had made to him about being her pimp, but now his curiosity had been ignited. He was wondering how much paper he could see from the 'hoe-stroll'.

*   *   *

MALIK AND RENNY were down at the spot on Penn Street getting ready to open up shop, he could see that she had been feeling really tense all day. Searching for his chance to finally become the champ, he opened up the negotiations.

"What's up, Renny," Malik probed, "You actin' like you need me to help you relieve some stress."

"What you talkin' 'bout, boy?" Renny said defensively.

"You know what I'm talkin' 'bout. I might be a young nigga, but ain't nothing slow about me except the way I talk. It's about time for you to give me a shot at the title."

Cook City Publishing

BY THE O.G. WISEMAN

Cook City Publishing

Malik grabbed Renny and pulled her close to him, his dick was rock-hard and she got wet instantly. Kissing her gently on the back of her neck, she couldn't resist.

"If you can handle this pussy young nigga, I'ma make you a champ," Renny uttered as she began to breathe heavily. Malik unbuttoned Renny's skirt and slid her right out of it. Seconds later, she was fully undressed. He kneeled down in front of her and began to kiss and lick the moistness between her legs. Renny grabbed Malik's shoulders and closed her eyes. "Ohh, baby, don't stop, don't stop. Right theeeeeeree! AAAHHHHH!" A couple of kisses and licks later, she was quivering and shaking. *'Damn, that felt good'*, Renny thought to herself. Malik was done with the foreplay; he got undressed and laid Renny down on the loveseat over in the corner of the room. Renny grabbed Malik and pulled him in front of her. Grasping his penis in her hand, she inserted it into her mouth and treated it like her favorite flavored popsicle. Massaging it with her luscious lips, she brought him to an extravagant climax; "Let it go baby! Let me taste how sweet you are," she moaned, as she licked his magic stick.
For the next 45 minutes, Renny had Malik on the ropes; he didn't know if he would be able to go the distance. Only halfway through the bout, he had six more rounds to go as Renny danced and played with him. The final round, she handed down her decision. "You put up a good fight, young scrappy, but I still hold the title!"

QUEEN BEE

*   *   *

THE COP with the grimacing face couldn't get Darlene off of his mind, he wanted her bad. He wanted her so bad that he would even set her up, sitting at his desk he brainstormed. In the holding pen on the 4th floor, Sharlene was locked up. She had been arrested after a sting operation went down on Second Street. The grimacing officer came up with a solution for getting rid of Darlene, and had Sharlene brought down to his office.

"If you want to get out of the trouble you're in, then you will do everything I need you to do," he said to her, as he looked at the rap sheet sitting in front of him. Nervously, Sharlene responded, "I can't afford to go to jail, sir. Please help me. I will do whatever I have to do." Pleased with Sharlene's agreement to help him, the officer with the grimacing face gave her the whole rundown, making sure she understood what had to be done.

*   *   *

POOH AND PEE-WEE had the whole projects high off of that 'Colombian Gold' reefer, everybody was coming through to cop a couple of bags. Because of the very low-key profile that they both kept, it was nearly impossible for anyone to tell the type of money that they were getting. Pee-Wee didn't even own a car. Most of the time he walked to wherever it was that he needed to go and if he wasn't walking, he either caught the bus or called a cab.

Pooh had an old black Chevrolet van with bald tires on it. It looked as if it wouldn't run for two miles without cutting off. Pooh and Pee-Wee were real close, they grew up together in the projects, nothing could separate their friendship. When they both got down with Dameka, they knew that it was on. Pooh and Pee-Wee were getting more money than any of their friends would ever see in their lifetime, and they were also fucking one of the baddest oldhead chicks in Cook City. The life they were living seemed to have come straight from a movie screen.

Cook City Publishing

*　　　　*　　　　*

THE SPEAKEASY had a nice little crowd for a Wednesday night. Danielle was kind of surprised to see how many people came through. When Ben Martin was at the jukebox playing a record, Sharlene and a derelict looking dark-skinned undercover officer came down the stairs and sat at the bar. Dressed in a flimsy, tan polyester two-piece suit, a pair of rust colored loafers and some Maxwell Smart dark tinted glasses, the officer, posing as one of Sharlene's tricks, cased the joint. Looking around the room he logged all of the

information into his brain. "Danielle, what's up, girl?"
Sharlene said cautiously. Danielle looked up from
pouring a shot of vodka and responded "I ain't seen you
in a while, where you been at, trick?" Sharlene and the
undercover officer jumped, the remark caught them off
guard. "I see you got a new piece of meat," Danielle
continued. "I know you ain't letting no nigga lock you
down!"

"Shit girl, ain't no nigga got a stroke that long.
If his money is long enough, he might be able to keep
me occupied for a minute, but after a while, I'm gone!"
They laughed. "What ya'll drinking?" Danielle asked. "I
know ya'll gonna spend some of that pussy money wit'
me."

"Give us two shots of Tiger Rose and two cans of
Budweiser," the undercover officer answered, pulling a
bankroll out of his suit jacket pocket.
Gypsy the car mechanic got up from the booth in the
back of the Speakeasy, drunk, talking shit. "We gonna
have us a muthafuckin' party tonight! I'm in the house,
and it's goin' down. I got a pocket full of money, and
I'm tryin' to spend it, I need me a shot of ass too!"
KC and the Sunshine Band came on the jukebox, and
Gypsy went wild, dancing and spinning around, he
was definitely in rare form. "Now we getting the party
started," he slurred, as he slipped and almost fell into
the crap table.

"Gypsy, if you don't sit yo' drunk ass down
somewhere, you goin' up outta here!" Danielle shouted
from behind the bar.

Cook City Publishing

"Who you callin' drunk? I ain't got started yet.
Give me a bottle of Wild Irish Rose so I can show you
what drunk really is!" Searching for his money, Gypsy
was staggering around bumping into chairs and stools,
knocking a few of them over.

"Nigga, I ain't sellin' you a bottle of nothin'!"
Danielle protested. "One more drink and you liable to
pass the fuck out!"

"Danielle, where's Dee at? I ain't seen my girl
in a while," Sharlene slid into the conversation, trying
to finish up the job that she had been sent there to do.
Danielle and the girls never talked about Darlene; so
she small talked around the question. "She around
somewhere. You know her, she stay on the move."
Forty-five minutes later, Sharlene and the undercover
officer left, their job had been done.

*   *   *

RAGS TO RICHES was a different story from Pooh
and Pee-Wee. These two playas were more than
flamboyant. Whenever they arrived on the scene,
everybody had to know it, they wore the flashiest suits
and drove the fanciest cars. When they spoke, they
made sure that everybody heard them. Making a grand
entrance in the front door of Gayzers' Bar and Grill on
Sixth Street, they were at it again. "Rags and Riches
just walked in the muthafuckin' door, so ya'll fake-ass
pimps hold on tight to yo' hoes. If not, we gonna make

Cook City Publishing

'em ours!" they chanted as they strolled through the crowd. "Set the bar up for every muthafuckin' body, if you ain't no real nigga or badass bitch, then you can't drink wit' us!" Riches yelled to make sure that he had been heard. Rags slammed two hundred-dollar bills down on the counter. "Somebody's leavin' wit Rags and Riches tonight! Which one of you hoes wanna be sucked and fucked in luxury? If you wanna be that special piece of ass, then step right up!"

When Rags and Riches left Gayzers' Bar and Grill that night, they had five badass hoes with them. On their way out of the door Rags turned around and laughed, "Anytime any of you lame-ass niggas wanna pick up some real game, then holla at us! We might let ya'll enroll in our certified school for hustlas, playas and pimps!"

*   *   *

THE NEXT morning at 8:00 a.m., the police arrested Danielle and Darlene for running a gambling spot and selling liquor without a license. The cop with the grimacing face was right there on the scene.

"Good morning, Mrs. Dennison," he said with a dumb-ass look. "I knew that we were destined to meet again."

"Kiss my ass, you lame ass toy cop!" Darlene responded, as they handcuffed her. Burning with envy, the officer with the grimacing face looked around at

Cook City Publishing

how beautiful Darlene's home was. He knew that in two lifetimes he would never be able to live the way that she did.

"I see the Speakeasy is paying off for you, huh? Well, it doesn't matter, because before it's all over you won't have any of this." Darlene smiled at him and rolled her eyes.

Downtown at the Police Station, the judge gave Danielle a $250,000 bail. He made up some bogus excuse about Darlene being a 'flight risk' as to why he was denying her bail. The rest of the girls flipped out. "What the fuck do you mean flight risk?" Renny screamed. "You know she ain't goin' no fuckin' where!" Dameka cursed, "I don't know what the fuck is goin on, but we gonna get to the bottom of this shit."

"If you ladies don't quiet down, then we have a place for you too," The Court Officer threatened. Coochie just sat back, taking in the whole scene, gathering her thoughts. As the police began to lead Darlene out through the back exit, Renny spoke again, "Don't worry, girl, we got ya' back to the end. If they think this shit's over then they better think again!" Coochie stood up in the back of the courtroom with tears in her eyes, watching Darlene being taken away. A half hour later, Danielle was being released and Darlene was on her way out to the Cook City County Jail in the back of the paddy wagon. Darlene had never been locked up before in her life, but she knew she could handle it. She was a tough chick and it would take more than a few days in jail to break her.

QUEEN BEE

Many thoughts were racing through Darlene's mind, but her main concern was Junior. She knew that he was getting big enough to take care of himself, but she still didn't like the fact that she didn't know how long she would be away from him. Although she was concerned, she wasn't worried because she knew that the girls would take care of him if he wanted or needed anything.

*   *   *

"MAN, SHIT is really startin' to change out here!" Pee-Wee said, counting another thousand stack and placing it to the side. "Niggas is startin to act real shady!"

"You know how that go, pimp!" Pooh replied, licking his thumb, recounting the stack that Pee-Wee had just counted, "Money breeds envy. When you start touchin' that real paper, even ya' best friend can become a potential enemy!"

"I be feeling a lot of that shit when certain niggas come around, or when I go over to Sunshine Park to see what's goin' down!"

"Them is some serious-ass feelin's, lil' homey. When you feel 'em like that, take heed to 'em. It's real when you can feel the heat from the next nigga! Pay attention to ya' senses, and don't ever allow yourself to be fooled by nothin' else!"

"Yo, you don't know how much I be hatin' that shit!"

Cook City Publishing

BY THE O.G. WISEMAN

Cook City Publishing

"Yeah I do! You don't think I be feelin' the same way? It frustrates me when I come around and niggas be on some funny shit! But I'm one step ahead of 'em already, because I know what it's hittin' fo'! Niggas is on some envious shit!"

"This is a serious game here, huh," Pee-Wee laughed. "In this one here, every playa is out to get the next one!"

"For the most part, that's how it is, baby," Pooh slid another stack to the side after counting it. "Every playa ain't the same, but you always gotta keep ya eyes on 'em as potential suspects for the Bowemont Cross!"

"Man, I don't like that shit!"

"Me either, but that's just the way it is. Hate it or love it, it is what it is!"

"I got something real nice for one of these niggas as soon as I think they gonna act up. If I'm lyin', I'm dyin'!" Pooh grabbed the joint out of the ashtray and lit it, "Look what just happened to Dee, this game ain't fair! Each individual playa by his or her own rules at the end of the day, the only winner is the one still left breathin' or roamin' the streets free!"

*　　　　　*　　　　　*

JUNIOR SAT on the couch with his eyes closed as Danielle told him about what had happened to his mother.

"Don't worry, everything is gonna be alright."

"When is she coming home?"

"I don't know exactly, but if you need anything just ask me or one of the girls, we will take care of it." After Danielle had left, Junior wiped his eyes, took a deep breath, and said a prayer for his mother.

*　　　　　*　　　　　*

Cook City Jail was more like a resort for Darlene rather than a prison. Even though she was locked up she had damn near everything that a person on the outside had. From the captains to the regular Correctional Officers, everybody knew who Darlene was. A few of the Correctional Officers had even been to the Speakeasy before. After Darlene's first couple of days in quarantine, she moved to a regular unit, which was N-Block. A lady officer named Mrs. Vial ran this particular section. Entering the unit, she greeted Darlene with open arms,

"How you doin', sugar? I'm sorry that we had to meet under these circumstances, but since we did, let's make the best of the situation." Darlene appreciated the kind gesture. Mrs. Vial gave Darlene the first cell up front, which was unoccupied. Anything that she needed help with, Mrs. Vial would do her best to assist her with, she held Darlene down on the first shift.

Drunk-ass C.O. Gordon looked out for her on the second shift, he was a cool-ass nigga. "Listen here, baby girl, I might not know you, but me and Phillip was real

Cook City Publishing

tight. Before I got this job eight years ago, I used to do a lil' hustlin'. Phillip always made it his business to see that I got what I was supposed to get for my money.

C.O. Gordon used to bring Darlene cooked meals, wine and even letters from Coochie and the girls, because there was a lot of things they couldn't talk about over the phone. The graveyard shift was the sweetest to Darlene. While most of the other inmates were asleep, Mrs. Wave would let her come out and do whatever she wanted to do. Most of the time, she would call and talk to her family. The only problem that Darlene had was with Dr. Gates. Everytime that she went to 'sick-call' or was called up front for medical reasons he would always give her a hard time. When she sat down and thought about how he treated her, she would swear there was a reason behind it. Most of Darlene's days went by fast, but some of them were a drag. Every morning she would look at the calendar and mark off each day until her preliminary hearing. Darlene's lawyer, Mrs. Smith, guaranteed that she would get bail. Darlene didn't know exactly what was going to happen but with all of the money that she was paying Mrs. Smith, something good had better happen.

*   *   *

ROLLING OVER in the bed, Rags patted Trisha on the ass. She was looking fine as a muthafucka, laying there naked, resembling a double of Debbie Allen in a

Cook City Publishing

heated sex scene of an X-rated movie. He was thirsty as hell and wanted a cold glass of iced water. He thought about waking her sweet ass up to go get him a cup, but he decided to get it himself.

Sliding into his black leather Ralph Lauren house slippers, Rags strolled towards the kitchen. Passing the large living room window of their Front Street apartment, which overlooked the Susquehanna River, he noticed two dark figures jacking his money green El Dorado up, and removing the customized Cadillac wheels. He rubbed his eyes to make sure he was seeing what he thought he was seeing, "What the fuck!"

Racing into Riches' bedroom and seeing Riches laid up in the bed with this Russian chick named Nimber, he tapped his homeboy on the shoulder, "Get the fuck up, nigga! It's some lames outside sittin' our shit on cinder blocks!"

Quickly dressing in his 100% cotton Pierre Cardin pajama set and his black leather Pierre Cardin house slippers, Riches grabbed the double-barreled pump shotgun that sat next to the bed, meanwhile Rags retrieved his .45 automatic from the storage closet. Strapped and ready for war, they exited the crib, moving in complete silence.

Tiptoeing up behind the dark figures dressed in hoodies, jeans and sneakers, Riches cocked his weapon, "Now what the fuck do you two fleas think we gonna do 'bout ya'll sittin' our shit on blocks?"

Startled, the two young kats looked back and saw nothing but a dark barrel staring them in the face.

Cook City Publishing

BY THE O.G. WISEMAN

"Don't say a damm thing!" Rags warned them. "Ya'll already in a fucked up situation! Don't make shit worse! Start putting my muthafuckin' tires back on my car!"

Without the slightest hesitation, the two figures complied, hastily dressing the El Dorado back up, placing it on all fours. Realizing that they were dealing with a couple of kids, Riches wanted to laugh, but figured it would be best if he carried out what he had planned for them. After the four wheels had been secured to the vehicle again, Rags ordered, "Now get the fuck up and walk across the street wit' ya' hands behind ya' head!"

Hurrying across the deserted intersection with Rags and Riches right behind them, the two young kats stopped at the bank of the river, which was approximately 10' deep.

"Now, ya'll got two choices!" Rags optioned, willing himself not to laugh, "Ya'll can either jump or take this hot shit we gettin' ready to put in ya'll!" Before the two kids could make up their minds, Riches shouted, "Fuck it!" BOOM! letting off a single shot into the air. Simultaneously, Rags and Riches kicked both of the young kats up the ass, sending them catapulting off the riverbank and into the river.

"Ya'll got off easy this time!"

"If we catch ya'll down here again, it's gonna get real sticky!"

With tears in his eyes, Rags dropped his gun to the ground and fell out laughing.

Cook City Publishing

QUEEN BEE

DAMEKA, DANIELLE, Renny and Coochie were handling their business as usual. The only exception was that they closed the Speakeasy down completely. With that part of the operation closed down. Danielle and Coochie opened up two more spots uptown. One was a weed spot down on Logan Street and the other was a coke spot up on Ross Street.

"With these two spots we should be able to triple what the Speakeasy was bringing' in," Coochie said as she wrote a couple of figures down on a piece of paper.

"Now we can focus on other things. I really felt that Speakeasy shit, but it was getting old."

"Yeah," Dameka responded. "We can open up another one somewhere else, and let somebody else run it. I got the perfect location too!"

Renny and Danielle were doing more thinking than anything; they knew that they couldn't afford any more run-ins with the police. They also knew that one mistake could end everything. Sitting behind the desk down in the office, Renny let her thoughts be known. "This shit is gettin' real serious Danielle, we gotta build walls around everything we have. If we don't somebody's gonna bring us down. You and Dee got this damm case hangin' over ya'll's heads. These crooked-ass cops are playin' for keeps."

"I'm feeling you, girl," Danielle said. We definitely

Cook City Publishing

gotta do somethin'. As a matter of fact, everybody that owe us gotta pay! We need all of ours and we need it now. Dee has been true to all of us, now we gotta be down for her. She should be outta there soon, but no matter what happens we gotta be down for her like she was down for us. She's my sister, but it goes way deeper than that. If it wasn't for her, I know none of us would have a lot of the things we got. Dee has only been locked up for a little over a week now, but it seems like she has been gone forever. We gotta make sure that she gets outta there! You, me, Dameka and Coochie is all she got!"

Renny hugged Danielle and whispered to her in a stern voice, "I will die for Dee, just as well as kill for her. When I speak, I speak from my heart. Somebody's gonna pay for this bullshit!"

Saturdays were Darlene's visiting days. She was only supposed to get 45 minutes of visiting time, but Captain Dunlap gave her an hour and a half. All of the girls always accompanied Junior on the visits. They laughed and talked about all of the things that were going on. It pained the girls to see Darlene dressed in her county jumpsuit. They had to coat their emotions though, because they knew she wouldn't accept crying. Darlene's happiest moments were seeing Junior and the girls, and her saddest ones were seeing them leave. The squad looked up to Darlene, and she knew that she had to be the perfect example and symbol of being strong under all circumstances. As each visit ended, Darlene

Cook City Publishing

would look each of them in the eye, hug and kiss them on both cheeks, and tell them that she loved them.

"We are too strong for them to break us!"

*   *   *

Coochie had found out through the grapevine that Sharlene had set Darlene and Danielle up. With tears in her eyes and revenge in her heart, she set out for retribution.

Friday night, after all of the bars had closed, Sharlene was walking down on Second Street trying to catch her next trick, when an old ragged brown van wit' two young guys in it, pulled up beside her. "What's goin' down, baby girl? We tryin' to have a lil' fun! How much is it gonna cost us?" the driver asked. That was Sharlene's cue. Quickly she stepped up to the van. When Sharlene got close enough, the side door suddenly open and somebody snatched her in. Coochie slammed her .44 magnum in Sharlene's face, while choking the shit out of her.

"You dumb bitch! I know you didn't think that we wasn't gonna find out about that bullshit that you did to Dee and Danielle. Now retribution must be paid!" Breaking free of Coochie's grip, Sharlene scurried to the back of the van.

"What the fuck you talkin' about? I ain't do shit to Dee and 'em!" Coochie followed her, and jumped dead on Sharlene's ass. Pooh and Pee-Wee turned up the

Cook City Publishing

Cook City Publishing

music so that they couldn't hear Sharlene screaming. Up behind Crooked Grill Road, they pulled into a shadowy pathway leading deep into the woods.

"PLEASE! PLEASE!" Sharlene begged, looking up from the ground where she had been dumped. Pooh and Pee-Wee grabbed her around the arms and started ripping off her skimpy clothes. Looking pitilessly down at Sharlene's naked and trembling body, Pooh yelled "Bitch! I know you didn't expect me to pay for that!" Pee-Wee broke out laughing wickedly.

After gagging and tying Sharlene to a tree, they burned her feet with a blowtorch. The pain was so dreadfully excruciating that she passed out. Pooh woke Sharlene back up to her gruesome reality by thunderously smacking her across the face with a large tree branch that lay beside the tree. The shattering blow awakened Sharlene, almost taking her head off of her shoulders. The grey masking tape that they had placed over her mouth muffled her blood-curdling screams.

"Wake the fuck up bitch!" Pee-Wee barked, untying her.

As Pooh and Pee-Wee marched Sharlene further into the woods, she hobbled and staggered all the way on her horrendously burned and mutilated feet. She winced and sobbed from the almost unbearable pain, until they reached their destination. A freshly dug six-by-twelve grave. They remorselessly and without any ceremony, tossed her into it. Hitting the moldy earth with a bonecrushing thud, Sharlene realized her end was mercilessly approaching, with no escape in sight she went into a panicked frenzy of muffled sobbing and begging through her gag. She kicked, jerked and flailed around in her new earth-bed. Her terror-filled eyes were blood red and bulged grotesquely from their wildly stretched sockets. Shovels full of dirt rained down on her for what seemed like an eternity.

"I don't think yo' stank ass is gonna survive this," Pooh spat. "Tell yo' daddy I said hi!" In the grim throes of panic and inaudible wailing, a horrorstricken soul and a pain wracked-body, Sharlene was buried very much alive.

*   *   *

THE PROJECTS was the perfect place to open up another Speakeasy, and Dameka knew it. Pooh and Pee-Wee handled the job with Coochie so well that the girls gave them this 'come-up' as a reward. Dameka showed them how things were supposed to be run and Pooh and Pee-Wee followed her orders to a 'T'. They already had the projects 'on lock' with the weed, now it was on another level with the beer, liquor and gambling. When the dice rolled, Pooh and Pee-Wee caught 'em, and Dameka got the cut for the house.

*   *   *

BY THE O.G. WISEMAN

Cook City Publishing

DARLENE AND DANIELLE went to their preliminary hearing, and just as they expected, the judge bounded their case over to the courts. Looking down at Darlene over the rim of his glasses, Judge Odom sucked his teeth, "I really don't want to give you bail Mrs. Dennison, but I'm going to grant you one. If you so much as jaywalk, I am going to lock your ass back up! You betta watch yourself, young lady!"
Judge Odom set Darlene's bail at half a million dollars. Three hours later, she was being released. The cop with the grimacing face was furious that Darlene had been granted bail; he hated her with an outrageous passion. He wouldn't rest until Darlene was back in jail for the rest of her life, or buried right next to her husband!Danielle, Dameka, Renny and Coochie were happy that Darlene was home, and they were ready to take the game to the highest level. All of them knew how much Darlene respected their hustle, and they wanted to show her that same passion. Darlene had many things on her mind. She was always thinking about the next move. She had big plans for Cook City, but first she would have to overcome her beef with the police. And in the process, she would have to handle all of the things getting ready to come her way.

CHAPTER EIGHT

THE CROSS

THE WEATHER out in Los Angeles was sunny and beautiful. The tropical palm trees made everyone feel like they were in a foreign country. Junior was amazed by the sights and the rest of the girls were just as excited. The small fleet of Cadillac baby-limousines that they traveled in made them feel like royalty. Darlene and Junior rode in the first car, while Coochie and Dameka followed closely behind in the second one and Renny and Danielle cruised remotely behind them, bringing up the rear. Arriving at the Hollywood Suites, they all smiled. Darlene had made their reservations before leaving Cook City. The hotel was 30 stories high. On the roof was an Olympic sized swimming pool that had a built-in wave machine, each of their rooms were connected. Looking down from the 25th floor made the people on the ground look like ants. When Junior saw the Movie Theater in the lobby of the hotel, he couldn't wait to get unpacked so he could catch one of the flicks being featured. Darlene and the girls wanted to go shopping and sightseeing. After they were all unpacked and settled in, Darlene called everybody into her room.

"If I didn't already say it before or ya'll don't already know how I really feel, I want ya'll to know that I appreciate the love and loyalty ya'll showed me for those couple of weeks that I was locked up. Ya'll are my family, and family means everything to me. When I say that I love ya'll, I mean it with all of my heart and soul. Ya'll kept it real wit' me, and it's a must that I keep it real wit' ya'll. For some reason, the police are out to get me, and I know this. That is why we must all watch one another's back at all times."

When Darlene paused, Renny stepped in; "It ain't nothin' that we won't do for you, Dee. If we gotta go to war wit' the police then that's what we will do. We don't want it to come to that, but if it does, then let my muthafuckin' pistol smoke!"

Dameka jumped up out of her seat and threw her hands in the air, "Why? I don't know, but that crooked face toy cop hates us!"

The rest of the girls didn't know about Darlene's history with the cop with the grimacing face. She couldn't pinpoint it, but there was something about him that still bothered her after all these years. Before it is all over, Darlene swore she was gonna put it all together.

QUEEN BEE

*　　　　　*　　　　　*

BACK IN COOK CITY, Rick Doggs was taking his game to the limit. He went up in a four story apartment complex on Seventh Street and paid all of the tenants to move out. The ones that didn't want to move, he evicted.

After the building had been vacated, Rick Doggs went through every apartment, cleaned them out and furnished each one with five tables and ten chairs. Each room had one table and two chairs in it. Nothing else occupied the place. From the floors to wall, the rooms were bare. The front entrance of the building had a steel cage welded to the door. All of the first floor windows were cemented up.

Rick Doggs' office was set up on the 4th floor. From his desk, he could see from one end of the block to the other, making it impossible for anyone to enter unannounced or unobserved. Unauthorized entry was forbidden. Every room in every apartment was used for getting high. Whenever a customer came to buy some coke from the building, they had the option of paying $10 extra to use one of the rooms or taking their package somewhere else. Rick Doggs drafted Malik as his partner for this mission. They were out to get money, much more money than any other hustla in the city. Rick Doggs ran things from the top floor, while Malik and his homeboy, Randy T., made sure that everything

Cook City Publishing

ran the way that it was supposed to from the ground up. Before activating his operation, Rick Doggs called a meeting up in his office.

"Ya'll two niggas gotta keep ya'll's eyes open at all times. What we are about to do has never been done before in Cook City, the streets is definitely gonna be talkin'. If ya'll niggas is tryin' to get money, then this is the spot."

"I'm feeling you Dogg," Malik responded. "This can become a muthafuckin' set-up."

Randy T. shook his head. "This can become a muthafuckin' empire!"

Sitting behind his desk, Rick Doggs continued, "If the police run down on us, they gonna try to make an example of us. Ya'll two niggas gotta hold me down. I'ma do the rest. If something happens, I'ma hold ya'll accountable."

All of them realized what they had on their hands, as long as they remembered the seriousness of what they were into, the sky was the limit. Rick Doggs was more than just a hustla. He was a supreme hustla, with his mind on his money and his money on his mind, he stayed focused.

Cook City Publishing

*   *   *

JUNIOR WAS having crazy fun out in Los Angeles. From the time he got up and put his clothes on, he was gone!

"Where you goin' now, boy?" Darlene asked as he came strolling by her room on his way out the door.

"Oh, what's up mom? I'm going upstairs to see what the pool area is looking like this morning."

"You be good and stay out of trouble."

Up on the roof in the pool area, Junior went into Mack mode. Older broads were sun tanning, exercising and lying around in the sun, if not naked, they were almost naked. So many flavors of women decorated the area that he wished he could have them all. Dipping through the lounge section where most of the women were laying, Junior heard a couple of whistles and mmm-mmm's. Reaching the spot where he decided to kick back, he was placed right next to a tantalizing Italian chick with long silky legs, long red hair that came down to her ass, and breasts that made the average man wish he was a baby again.

Placing his Cartier sunglasses on his face, Junior removed his shirt, revealing his massive and sculptured abs. Silence filled the air as heads turned. The Italian broad looked up at Junior and cocked her left leg up in her lounge chair. From where Junior was standing, all he saw was pussy. "Damn!" he said to himself, while focusing on the thick piece of lamb chop in front of him. Breaking the silence, the Italian chick spoke, "Would you be kind enough to rub some suntan lotion on my back?"

"It would be my pleasure," Junior answered.

Lying on her stomach she casually inquired, "What's your name?"

Cook City Publishing

BY THE O.G. WISEMAN

Cook City Publishing

Softly rubbing the suntan lotion into her back and shoulders he replied, "My name is Junior, and yours?"

"My name is Lovey," she responded in a strong Italian accent, "My, Junior, you have very soft hands." From the looks of Lovey, Junior figured that she was about 25 or 26. He knew that she had no idea how old he was. But then again, he wondered if she really cared. As Junior began rubbing the suntan lotion on Lovey's lower back he couldn't help but notice how toned her ass was. Lightly rubbing up against it, his dick got harder than algebra. While he was engaging in the act with Lovey, Coochie walked up beside him with a jealous look in her eyes.

"I see you got your hands full, boy!" Junior looked up at Coochie and smiled, sensing her disapproval, "What's up Cooch?"

"We're about to leave, if you are coming with us you better come on!" Before Junior could say another word, Coochie turned and walked away.

"I think you better go, cutie."

"What's up wit' me seeing you later on?" Junior asked as he stood up. "I'm trying' to see how fluent my Italian is."
Lovey blushed scarlet; "My room number is one twelve. I'll be waiting."

"I'll be there for my lessons at about ten thirty tonight." I hope that you are an experienced teacher, I may be a little rusty."
Junior touched Lovey softly on the inside of her right thigh, and then he was gone.

QUEEN BEE

*   *   *

RAGS AND RICHES were playing their part; they were stacking paper like Russell Simmons. The only bad moves they were making were unnecessarily creating enemies on their road to the riches. A lot of fake-ass hustlas, wanna-be playas, and part-time pimps were really beginning to dislike them. When it came to the hoes out on the streets, all they wanted to do was fuck 'em. Ever since their encounter with Coochie, they learned a valuable lesson. They kept it strictly business and dicked 'em down like Jim Brown. Rags and Riches were getting so much pussy, that every hoe in town was talking about them. When Joe-Joe's hoes mentioned their names, he put his foot dead in their ass.

"I'm gonna murder them two lame ass birds, don't nobody fuck wit' my hoes without my permission!" Saturday night, Times Hotel and Bar was the place to be. The corners of Fourteenth and Regina Streets all the way up to Fifteenth Street were flooded with people. All of the baddest hoes in Cook City were out getting that trick money right. Dope fiends and crackheads were scrambling around trying to get high. The pimps were pimping, and the playas were playing. Cars of every make and model laced the streets, bumper to bumper and double-parked. Rags and Riches pulled up in their bronze colored 190E Class Mercedes Benz. Joe-Joe was lurking in the darkness, waiting for them. After Rags

Cook City Publishing

parked their car in the parking lot across the street from the bar, Joe-Joe stepped out of the alleyway holding a pretty-ass longbarreled chrome .45 that sparkled as the streetlight reflected off of it. Before making his move, Joe-Joe made sure that his timing was right.

Just as Riches opened up the car door to get out, Joe-Joe fired three rapid shots at him. One of the bullets caught him in the right arm; ripping through his limb.

"What the fuck!" Rags shouted, as he reached into his coat and pulled out his 9-millimeter handgun. Before Rags could react, Joe-Joe was firing on them again. This time he shattered the front windshield of their car, and hit Rags in the stomach. A blizzard of shattered glass flew in every direction. Rags slammed back into the driver's seat, clutching his abdomen. Joe-Joe was preparing to fire again when Rags and Riches both rolled out of the car and hit the ground. When they came up, they came up firing. Rag's was holding his stomach, but he was gunning for Joe-Joe.

The exchange of gunfire between the three of them was deafening, people were running, screaming and trampling one another. Rag's fired three more shots at Joe-Joe, taking chunks out of the bricks above his head. While Joe-Joe was ducking the shots from Rags, Riches caught him twice in the chest. The impact from the bullets pushed him up against the wall; knocking him to the ground. Joe-Joe still had his gun in his hand. Presuming that Joe-Joe was dead, Rags and Riches ran up on him with their guns drawn. Just as Rags and Riches reached the other side of the street, Joe-Joe

Cook City Publishing

raised up with the last ounce of strength that he had left in his body, and let off three shots killing both of his approaching assailants instantly.

The first shot hit Riches in the neck, twisting his head around to the point where it looked as if it had snapped off. The second and third shots drove Rags staggering back into the street where he collapsed, after being hit in the stomach again. In that very instant Joe-Joe's head fell backward, hit the pavement and he breathed his last breath.

*　　　*　　　*

THE WHOLE gang was having fun out in L.A. It was a whole new experience for all of them, Darlene and the girls went shopping every chance they got. They even rode out to Hollywood and visited the world famous 'Hollywood Stars Walk of Fame' in front of Mann's Chinese Theatre. They sighted all types of celebrities and even took pictures with them. Their most memorable moment was when they met the legendary Redd Foxx, he had all of them laughing. When he did his impression of Fred Sanford, from the hit television show 'Sanford and Son' that took the cake!

*　　　*　　　*

"HEY, RICK DOGGS!" Shanda Banks purred strutting up on him, dressed scantily in a red Jordache

Cook City Publishing

jean skirt with only a white, lacey Victoria's Secret like bra up under the half buttoned up matching jean jacket. The opened-toed calf-length Nine-West boots that she sported intensified her enticing look. "What it be like ma?" Rick Doggs responded, sipping on a cold glass of orange juice.

"I been watchin' you all night. It look like you need a lil' company!"

"Oh yeah? Whatever gave you that idea?" Looking at Rick Doggs with lust in her eyes, Shanda licked her lips, "It's Friday night, you sittin' over here by ya'self and I only seen you talk to one girl all night!" Taking in Shanda's response, Rick Doggs smirked, "Company is the last thing I'm lookin' for, baby! On the real, I'm lookin' for some more Abraham Lincolns and Andrew Jacksons to go home wit'!"

"So what you sayin'? You don't want somethin' soft like this to cuddle up wit'?" Shanda turned around and poked her ass out.

"If you take me home, I know you gonna keep me!" Rick Doggs laughed, "If I take you home, I'ma miss Andrew and Abe!"

"I'ma let you think about it for a minute before I walk off. Once I'm gone, I'm gone!"

"Ain't nothin' to think about, ma'! I can get a piece of ass anywhere! I ain't out here for that! I'm out here to get me some money! I ain't knockin' you fo' ya' pitch, but it ain't my speed! Don't get me wrong, you lookin' good as a mutha', but I ain't in it for that! If you do catch one of these lames out here wit' they

Cook City Publishing

pants down, make sure he got a pocket full of money! If you don't get it all, send him my way!"

Raising his glass up to a disappointed Shanda, who was standing with a confused look on her face, Rick Doggs downed the rest of his orange juice, "Always remember that if it don't make dollars ma', then it don't make sense!"

*   *   *

AFTER A LONG day of shopping and sightseeing in Hollywood, Darlene and her gang all headed back to Los Angeles. While they were riding along some of the streets that Phillip had once told Darlene about, she got teary eyed and wished she could have shared this experience with him. Closing her eyes and resting her head back on the seat, she heard Phillip's voice say, *"It's okay baby."* She smiled and pulled Junior close to her. At 10:35p.m. that night, Junior was down in Lovey's room. Class was in session. She couldn't help get him out of his clothes fast enough.

"Slow down baby," Junior smiled as Lovey unzipped his pants. "We got all night."

"I can't help myself daddy," she responded eagerly. "Since the first time you touched me earlier today, I knew that I had to have you." Because of how hot Lovey was, Junior decided to have some fun with her, he fucked her in every position he could think of. When he had tried them all, he tried them again. Lovey

Cook City Publishing

was a live wire, anything that Junior wanted of her, she was more than willing to do.

"Is this the way you like it, Daddy?" were her favorite words. She was an All-American pro when it came to sucking dick, no matter how much Junior came, she always wanted more. One time, he came so much that she started choking. Removing his penis from her mouth, cum shot all over her face and hair. Junior wanted to laugh, but played it off and acted as if he was concerned.

Lovey had never had any man do things to her that Junior had done, and she was more than open for discussion. She was hit, split and down with it. With her sweet Italian accent, Lovey looked up into Junior's eyes. "Can't you stay here in L.A. with me, Daddy? I will do whatever's necessary to take care of you." Amused by Lovey's statement, Junior said, "Come on now, baby, I gotta go back home wit' my family. If I told my mother I was stayin' out here, she would have a heart attack."

As Lovey began to pout, Junior licked circles around her hard nipples.

"Please stay with me Daddy!"

All night Lovey pleaded and begged Junior, she had fallen madly in love with him. In the morning when Junior told Lovey he had to go, he kissed her on the cheek and wiped a lonely tear from her eye. Back upstairs in his hotel room, he couldn't stop thinking about how that Italian chick went crazy over him. He

Cook City Publishing

knew that if he really wanted to, he could be a boss pimp. He was definitely feeling it; but there was one final test that he would have to pass. (Coochie)

*　　　　　*　　　　　*

THE NEW COKE spot that Rick Doggs had opened up was bigger than Rosey Grier. Everyday the money seemed to get bigger and better; the sniffers and shooters were partying 24/7. If their money was really right, Malik would let them bring some hoes up in the spot. It was a dream come true for anybody who bought coke and wanted to get high right there. If business went really well, Randy T. would give all of the customers a free half-gram with anything they bought. That was their way of showing the customers that they appreciated their business and it always kept them coming back. Nobody in the city had coke as raw as Rick Doggs did. The same way that he got it was the same way that he sold it, straight off the triple beam. Since the first day the coke spot opened, word spread quickly. If you were lookin' for some raw shit and you wanted a place to get high, 'The White House', down on Seventh Street was your best bet.

Rick Doggs didn't like much attention, he knew all to well the trouble it would bring. He also knew that he had two cannons downstairs holding him down, and they wouldn't hesitate to leave a lame-ass nigga leaking.

Cook City Publishing

BY THE O.G. WISEMAN

*   *   *

THE NIGHT before it was time for them to fly back to Cook City, Darlene took all of them to a concert. Kool and The Gang, De Barge, Rick James and The Gap Band were performing. The concert was a sold out event. They saw Richard Roundtree, Jimmy Walker, a young Magic Johnson and a whole array of other celebrities. The gang's last night in Los Angeles was more than a party; it was a Mardi Gras. After a week of partying and lots of sun, it was time for them to go home. They all looked forward to getting back to business, but they had no idea of the events that would take place once they got back to the streets of Cook City. Banchey came to see Darlene as soon as they got home. "Hey baby girl! I'm glad to see you made it back safely. I was beginnin' to worry about you, you been havin' a lot of drama in ya' life lately."

"Yeah, I know," Darlene responded, kind of amused at seeing Banchey. "Everything will be okay though. I'ma make sure of that!"

Banchey and Darlene talked for about half an hour, and agreed to meet later on that evening at 8:30. Banchey was hoping that Darlene would open up to him, but it wasn't her heart that he wanted her to open up, it was her legs.

*   *   *

187

QUEEN BEE

The rest of the girls went straight to work, they were anxious to see what had happened in the short time that they were gone. More importantly, they wanted to collect their money that they had out in the streets. Renny rode around a little before going over to the spot, when she didn't see Malik, she opened up shop and handled her business. Danielle quickly heard about the spot that Rick Doggs had opened up. She couldn't believe it.

Turning the corner on Seventh Street, Rick Doggs spotted Danielle's car before she pulled up in front of the spot. Walking up to the front entrance, Malik buzzed Danielle in.

"What's up slim? I didn't know ya'll was back, I know Renny is looking for me."

Observing the set-up in astonishment, Danielle asked, "Where's Rick Doggs' crazy ass at?"

"He's upstairs on the fourth floor, go ahead up and holla at him."

Getting off the elevator, Danielle walked straight to the back apartment where Rick Doggs was expecting her. He couldn't help showing how pleased he was to see her. "What it be like baby doll?" Rick Doggs asked, hugging Danielle so tight that she could barely breathe.

After he let her go, she gave him one of those long wet, juicy kisses. "I see you done stepped up ya' game since I been gone."

"Yeah baby girl. I hope you proud of the moves I made. It's definitely on another level."

"I'm always proud of you sugar, your moves

188

always make me happy."

As Danielle sat down on the black leather sofa, Rick Doggs stepped into the closet and came back out with a big green duffel bag. "This is for you slim, if it ain't about dollars, then it don't make sense," he said as he sat it down in front of her. The duffel bag was filled with money. Opening it up, Danielle was more than satisfied.

"Now, this is what the fuck I'm talkin' about!" Before Danielle could speak again, Rick Doggs slid up on her and kissed her passionately. Within seconds, they were both naked, having wild sex. Rick Doggs was Danielle's number one hustla, and he was also her number one playa in bed.

Cook City Publishing

*   *   *

Dick Dastardly ran up on Coochie with the news about Rags and Riches. "Yeah, baby girl, them niggas had a vicious shootout, Joe-Joe killed both of 'em. He died too!"

The story shocked Coochie briefly, but she quickly regained her composure. She knew not to show any feelings in front of Dick Dastardly.

"Damn, I'm sorry to hear that," she said smoothly, maintaining her stern face. "I guess that's the way life goes."

Coochie peeled off a hundred dollar bill, and hit Dick Dastardly off, then she rode away. She was very disappointed in Rags and Riches. "How could them niggas let that lame-ass Joe-Joe get the drop on 'em?" she said to herself. Rags and Riches were gone. Although it was hard to accept, she knew she had to let them go. In her own freaky little way, Coochie had love for them, but they slipped up and got sent on their way. But the hustle had to go on and by any means, it would.

*   *   *

Dameka went straight out to the projects to holla at Pooh and Pee-Wee about how pleased she was with them as well. The Speakeasy had doubled in profits, the weed was still being burned and the coke game was off the meat rack. Looking at her two young hustlas, Dameka commended them, "Yeah, ya'll niggas is definitely doin' it the right way. I got something real special for ya'll later on tonight."
Pooh and Pee-Wee smiled, with pussy on their brains.
"I can't wait," Pee-Wee said as he rubbed Dameka's ass.
"I know that's right," Pooh added. "It's been a while since I tasted something sweet!" They laughed.

*   *   *

Darlene and Banchey went through the whole night without a problem, Banchey was a perfect gentleman. He wanted to touch Darlene real bad but he restrained himself. Every time he looked at her in the tight yellow skirt-suit that she was wearing, he wanted to rip it right off of her, and give her what she hadn't had since Phillip had been murdered. But what Banchey didn't know was that Darlene had already decided that she was going to let him taste her honey that night. As Banchey was preparing to take Darlene home, she grabbed his hand and whispered in a soft voice, "Since you been such a good boy tonight, I'm going to give you something sweet to eat for desert." Banchey couldn't believe the words he was hearing. Smiling, he responded, "I'm sure it'll be my favorite."

At the Clover Leaf Motel, Banchey and Darlene did something that she hadn't done in over five years. Banchey was still baffled about her decision to give him a shot of pussy, he treated it like it was stamped fragile, they spent at least an hour and forty-five minutes in lustful acts of intercourse. At times, Darlene was really into it, but there were moments when she wanted to tell him to stop. After they had changed positions for about the forth and fifth time and Banchey was about to get on top of her again, Darlene started crying, "Wait, I can't do this no more."

"What?" Banchey asked as he looked down at her. "What's wrong, Dee?"
Darlene got up and headed for the shower. "You wouldn't understand," she managed to say in between sobs. "I love Phillip so much that I can't do this. I feel dirty and mixed up."

"Phillip is gone, Dee!"

"Phillip will never be gone! He will always live inside of me!"

Hearing how Darlene really felt, Banchey got up, got dressed, and took her home. He finally realized that Phillip still held the key to Darlene's heart, even though he would never again be able to use it. Banchey wanted to say a lot of things to Darlene, but he felt it best not to. He didn't want to just fuck her; he wanted to make her a part of his life. He wanted to fill the void that Phillip had left. Banchey felt that he had done all he could do to get with Darlene and he still fell short, so he dropped her off and kept it rolling.

Inside the house, Darlene made sure that she was alone. She sat down on the couch, placed her head in her lap and cried. She was hurting inside, she cried so hard that at times she felt her heart was going to burst through her chest. Her last tear came when she heard Phillip's voice again. *"Dry ya' eyes, baby girl. It's okay, I know how much you love me."*

*   *   *

JUNIOR AND FRO hooked up as soon as Junior got back from L.A. Fro showed Junior all of the money he had made since Junior had been gone. Then he put Junior down with everything that was going on in the streets. They kicked it for a minute, smoked a joint

Cook City Publishing

and then bagged up some weed to sell. Riding down Third Street in Junior's brand new powder blue El Dorado, Junior and Fro spotted this lame ass nigga in a grey goodwill suit, choking the shit out of Lisa. Junior slammed on the breaks and jumped out.

"Nigga, I don't know who the fuck you is, but if you don't get yo' hands off my bitch, I'ma break yo' muthafuckin' neck!"
The lame in the gray suit whirled around, "Yo bitch?" Nigga, this is my bitch!"
Catching her breath, Lisa scrambled over to Junior's side. "I'm Junior's hoe," she gasped, "I was wonderin' when he was comin' back to get me!"
Infuriated, the lame in the gray suit pulled his pistol and fired at Junior. Dipping to the left and brandishing his own gun, Junior's reflexes were so quick that Fro didn't even see Junior move. Junior caught the lame in the gray suit twice. Once in the chest, and once in the stomach. Piercing his heart and ruining his intestines, the shots knocked him off of his feet. Opening his mouth to try and beg for his life, POP! Junior hit him dead in the head. Blood splattered all over Fro and Lisa's clothes. The lame in the gray suit left the world the same way he had entered it: brainless.

*   *   *

SITTING BEHIND her desk, Darlene thought about young Rick Doggs and the major accomplishments during the short time that she and her mob were out of town. With power moves such as the ones he had made, she could easily envision him running the city, hands down. She was glad that he had decided to remain loyal to her and her cause. She knew that at any given time, if the thought crossed his mind, he could venture out on his own and become a major problem for her crew. The mere thought of it turned her stomach; she would hate to have to dispose of such an good asset. Darlene never really dealt with him, she always remained respectfully a third party; Danielle took care of whatever needed to be done as far as transactions with Rick Dogg's were concerned. From day one, Darlene had a good vibe about dealing with the young hustla from New York. In fact, she welcomed her sister's idea with open arms, she was curious with what he had to offer her and her squad in the form of a different breed of a hustla.

*   *   *

Danielle gave him the green light, after giving him a shot of ass, and then turned him loose on the city. Just as she had envisioned, it all paid off. Never in a million years did any of them guess that Rick Doggs was going to be such as asset to their organization. When he first joined the team, he was just a pup with potential, now he was full grown with a dangerous bite. Because the main pieces of her team were basically made up of four women, Darlene welcomed the presence of a strong young male with ambition into her circle. There were also a few others, but none of them impressed Darlene the way Rick Doggs did. The fact that she knew that he cared about her sister made her feel him all the more. Swirling around in her swivel chair, facing the picture of Phillip gracing the rear wall, Darlene looked up at her long lost, but never forgotten love and faintly smiled. "I know if you were around you would like this young kat, baby! In many ways, he reminds me of you. I think he gonna do real good under my guidance. And even more, I think he's gonna make a fine husband for Danielle one day!"

Cook City Publishing

*　　　　*　　　　*

Coochie stepped up her game ten levels after she got back. With her two main hustlas gone, she had to run with the ball. All of Rag's and Riches' old clientele became hers. Coming through the door of any joint in the city, everybody from hustlas to cokeheads waited in line to see her. If a nigga wasn't down with Coochie or tied to her in some way, then he probably wasn't seeing too much money. From the Sixth Street strip to the Southside slums, Coochie was running the show. There wasn't a bitch in the streets that could touch her. She was the baddest thing in Cook City, second only to her mentor, the baddest of the baddest bitches, Darlene.

*　　　　*　　　　*

QUEEN BEE

RENNY AND DARLENE had heads turning when they stepped through the door at the Steelton Elks. Wall-to-wall, the place was packed. Parliament was spinning up in the D.J. booth and the system sounded nice and clear. Renny was done up in a soft gray and white rabbit fur coat, with rabbit fur boots to match. Darlene had on a dark cherry sheepskin shawl with a sheepskin turban, and a pair of cherry colored 'gator boots with 6" heels. If money made these two bitches, then they were definitely made. Anybody with any sense could tell that these two broads were born with style. Sitting in the back of the Elks at their regular table, Darlene and Renny were enjoying themselves while watching everybody else dance. Out of nowhere, three jealous hoes walked up to their table talking shit. Of the trio, the tall fish-eyed, one spoke first. "You two bitches think ya'll own the world. Well, I'ma let ya'll know that I don't give a fuck who ya'll are or how much money ya'll got!"

Simultaneously amazed and pissed at the woman's audacity, Darlene and Renny looked at one another. The heavy-set brown-skinned chick with big lips stepped in, "Ya'll actin' like ya'll pussy don't stank, sittin' back here like ya'll run the joint. Ya'll lucky I don't fuck one of ya'll up!"

Like a dog on a cat's ass, Renny stood up and slapped the shit out of the heavy-set chick. The sparks started flying. Pulling her straight razor out of her pocketbook, Darlene went to cutting some ass up right away. The first strike was across the forehead of the heavy-set

Cook City Publishing

Cook City Publishing

broad. "Aahhhh!" Blood gushed down her face as Darlene grabbed her by the hair and flung her to the floor. Immediately the D.J. cut the music off and the crowd scattered, helter-skelter for the front, and back exits. Renny was punching and kicking the tall fish-eyed chick anywhere that she could. It was definitely a one-sided fight. Darlene cut the third broad across the back as she tried to run, "Aahhhh!" Falling forward, she tumbled into a row of chairs.

"You hoes think this is a game, don't ya'll?" Well, ya'll fuckin' wit' the right bitches now!" Darlene screamed.

The bouncers wanted to break the ruckus up, but they knew how Darlene and Renny got down, and they didn't want that trouble on their hands. So, they just laid back and waited for the fireworks to end. When Darlene and Renny finally did finish, the three hating-ass hoes that stepped to them were running, screaming and scrambling to get away. Although Darlene and Renny had to kick some ass that night, they had a lot of fun. They knew that a lot of other bitches felt the same way that the three freshly vanquished hoes felt. But they didn't care because if anybody else tried to disrespect them in any way, they too would get just what these three got.

"They ass', thoroughly, kicked!"

CHAPTER NINE

TIME OUT

AT 1:45a.m. Thursday night, a beat up brown Toyota Corolla pulled into Downey school's parking lot down on Cameron Street. From where the car was parked, the occupants of the vehicle could see everything going in and out of Pooh and Pee-Wee's Speakeasy. Emerging from the car, a perfectly built red-boned chick, with more breasts and thighs than Kentucky Fried Chicken, walked over and entered the spot. Ten minutes later, she came back out. Standing behind the bar pouring Rob-O a drink, Pee-Wee was high as a muthafucka. Pooh, Ram, Dave, Maxx and Cliff were standing around the Crap Table Pee-Wee rolling the dice to see which one of them was going to shoot first.

Without a warning, Crash!...the back door flew off its hinges. Four young kats, wearing masks, barged into

Cook City Publishing

the spot holding crazy heat. The first one through the door shot Cliff in the Chest, lifting his body up onto the crap table. "OH SHIT!" instantly, Pooh dropped to the ground and cocked his .38. Ram, Dave and Maxx all tried to break for cover. The second and third kats through the door shot up everybody; hitting Dave in the leg, killing Maxx with a blow to the head, and pushing Ram across the room with a deadly back shot.
It sounded like the whole projects was under attack. While all of the shooting was going on, Pee-Wee was able to make it to his pistol. Pooh fired at the first kat that came through the door, but missed him.Before he could get off another shot, the fourth assailant appeared and hit him twice in the right side, taking a section out of his body. Slumping over, Pooh fell to the floor. Horrified by the death of his longtime homeboy, Pee-Wee recklessly let off four shots, ripping into one of the robbers shoulders. As the wounded stick-up man began to fall, he blasted back. All three shots jolted Pee-Wee's frail little frame, flipping him backwards over the bar, extinguishing his life. Walking around to each one of the victims, the stick-up kids began shooting them again, making sure that they were all dead, leaving nothing less than a bloodbath. Quickly, but thoroughly, the robbers searched the Speakeasy from top to bottom, finding all of the drugs and money. In the refrigerator, they hit the jackpot: They found all the cabbage. The stick-up kids had gotten all they had come for, and before it was all over, they would get even more.

Cook City Publishing

QUEEN BEE

*   *   *

DARLENE AND RENNY were at the house watching Prism on T.V. when Renny told Darlene she wanted to talk to her. "Dee, I want you to know how much I appreciate you bringing me out here and giving me a chance to live a better life. Ever since we were kids, I always looked up to you. When you would come to visit my mom and me in the summer, I never wanted you to leave. Damn near everything I know I learned from you. You might be my cousin, but to me you are more like a sister. I always had it but you gave me my style. No matter what happens, always remember that I love and respect you. You, Dameka, Danielle and Coochie are my family, and I will do anything for ya'll! When I said that I would die for you, I meant that! When I said that I would kill for you, I meant that even more!"
As Renny continued to talk, she began to cry. Darlene grabbed Renny, put her right arm around her shoulder and said, "You don't have to tell me how much you love me girl, you show me everyday."

The next day, Junior overheard his mother and his aunt Dameka talking about what had happened to their spot out in the projects, hearing his aunt cry really upset him. Picking up the phone, he called his homeboy, Fro. "Yo, we got some bizness to handle. See if you can find out who hit up Pooh and Pee-Wee's spot out in the

Cook City Publishing

projects."

"I got you, homey. I'm right on top of that shit!"
The line went dead. Three hours later they had what
they needed. Fro found out that it was four young
niggas from Pooh and Pee-Wee's projects that had hit
them up. He found out where they hung out and the
whole nine.

After the plan had been put together, Fro and Junior
strapped up and went to handle the situation. Looking
over at Fro, Junior eyes said. "You know exactly what
we gotta do." Fro replied with a look in his eyes that
said, "I got you homey, anything that moves gets hit!"
At the top of the hill on the other side of the projects,
Junior parked his car on corner of Fifteenth and Herr
Streets, next to the church. Before getting out of the
vehicle, he and Fro checked and reloaded their weapons.
Their next move was into the woods that led through
the projects to the heart of the circle where everybody
hung out.
Junior and Fro crept through the path and stopped right
before the opening. Junior analyzed the scene carefully,
    "You see them two niggas right there, and that
nigga over there, and the lame right there? Them is
the niggas we want," he said as he pointed out each
individual.
    "I got you homey."
The crowd in the circle was standing around drinking
beer, listening to music and smoking reefer. As they
watched, two of the girls put on a little dance show, one

Cook City Publishing

of whom was the red-boned chick that had set Pooh and Pee-Wee up.

Junior and Fro stepped out of the woods. With no warning at all. BOOM! Junior struck one of the kats in the back, knocking him forward into a parked car, killing him instantly. The rest of the lames pulled out their guns and started ducking, trying to identify the source of the shooting. The girls were screaming, hollering and panicking. From another direction, Fro caught another one of the lames in the face, pushing his life beyond existence. The two remaining kats were now utterly baffled. They didn't have the slightest clue where the unknown assassins were located. From the blind side Junior crept up on them.

"What comes around goes around you lame-ass niggas!" Leaving them both in a permanent state of unawareness. All that the noise the two girls were making made Fro even madder than he already was. So, he decided to give them something that would definitely keep them quiet.

The last shot came from Junior. BOOM! Killing the music, and knocking the radio off of the top of the wall.

The cop with the grimacing face was investigating all of the killing sprees that had taken place in the last few months. Every time he got some information, Darlene and her crew's name came up. "If it's the last thing that I do before I leave this world, I'm gonna get that Darlene Dennison. One of us has got to go!" he said to himself, "Cook City ain't big enough for the both of us!"

Cook City Publishing

BY THE O.G. WISEMAN

Cook City Publishing

*   *   *

DANIELLE WAS really starting to feel Rick Doggs, she had never been in love before. Feeling that things were starting to get too deep, she went to talk to Darlene.

"Dee, I don't know what to do. I'm really feelin' this young kat, but I don't want to set myself up for failure. Plus, I remember you tellin' us to never allow our emotions to get involved."
Darlene asked in a concerned voice, "How does Rick Doggs feel?"

"I know that he is feelin' me too, but I don't know how strong it is. Sometimes I want to ask him, but I don't know how. You know he is nine years younger than I am."
Darlene took Danielle's right hand and placed it in hers, "If Rick Doggs is feelin' you, then you will be able to feel it. Don't be afraid, girl! Ever since you met him you showed him love. If he is really a real nigga, then he will show you that same type of love in return."

*   *   *

Late Monday night all of the girls were out handling their business. The only one at home was Coochie, hearing the front door slam, she came downstairs to see who it was. Coochie was dressed in only a hot pink see-through nightgown. You could see everything from her titties to the finely trimmed hairs on her pussy. With two long braids hanging from the sides of her head, she looked just like a pretty, young sqaw. Adoring the beautiful creature standing before him on the staircase, Junior thought that he was dreaming.

"Damn Cooch! lookin' real sexy tonight. If you knew what I knew, you would hurry back up those stairs!"

Staring at Junior for a moment, with one hand on her hip, and the other on the banister, Coochie replied "Boy, if you knew, what I knew you wouldn't be talkin' like that!"

Junior slid up on Coochie and stuck his right hand up under her nightgown. Feeling the moistness between her legs, he took his other hand and palmed her ass. The moment that Coochie had been wondering about for so long had finally come.

"Boy you just don't know what you got yourself into, I told you these waters are too deep for you to swim in."

"I thought you knew Cooch," Junior bragged, "I got a mean backstroke!"

Grabbing Junior by the hand, Coochie led him upstairs to her room. Once there, she laid him down on her bed and stood over him. Unfastening his pants, she slid them off.

"Just lay there," she whispered.

Mounting herself on top of Junior, she moved up and

Cook City Publishing

down in slow pleasurable motions. Junior couldn't believe how good it felt, he had never had any pussy on this level. From the back and then facing him, Coochie came twice. Each climax was more intense than the last. Junior rolled her over on her stomach and began to kiss the insides of her thighs.

"Ooooohhh, that feels good Junior" Coochie moaned as she clutched the sides of the bed. When she couldn't take it anymore, Junior entered her, slowly thrusting his dick into her deep velvet ocean. Every time he reached the point of climaxing he would pull his dick out of her pussy and start licking and kissing all over her ass.

"Don't stop Junior, don't stop!" Coochie whined and hissed. Inserting himself inside of her again, he let it all go. Simultaneously they experienced the flow. Coochie shook and shivered like she was doing a brand new dance. Junior released himself and smiled. Turning her head and looking back at him from behind, Coochie muttered, "Ooooohhh shit! Boy, you better not tell nobody about this. If your mom ever found out, I would never hear the end of it!"

"Be easy Cooch, it's all good," Junior responded confidently. "Just remember how strong this young kat's dick game is. This pussy is mine."

"What?"

"Yeah Cooch, I'ma real P.I.M.P.," Junior laughed.

*　　　　　*　　　　　*

Cook City Publishing

RICK DOGGS had the hustle in a vise grip, he had more coke customers than he thought existed in Cook City. Even though the girls were doing their thing, nothin' could come close to the business that the 'White House' down on Seventh Street was doing. He had started renting out whole apartment units to certain kats to have their coke parties, charging $200 a night for the entire set-up. Anything that they wanted, he had for them. He even knew a couple of girls that would come through and party with the clientele, for the right price. The streets were all that Rick Doggs knew, and he had loved them more than anything else…until he met Danielle.

*   *   *

AFTER POOH and Pee-Wee's murder, Dameka started having different thoughts about the game, needing to talk to someone about the way she felt she went to Coochie.

"Cooch, have you ever thought about leaving the game alone?"

"Why you ask me that?"

"Cause I been thinkin' about the case that Dee and Danielle got."

"I ain't gonna say that I never thought about it, but this is my life. Dee and Danielle got that punk-ass case, but that don't scare me…" Dameka interrupted

Cook City Publishing

BY THE O.G. WISEMAN

Coochie,

"Don't you feel that we have made enough money? We have been doin' this shit for close to six years. Nothing lasts forever girl! How long do you think this shit is gonna last? Look at all of the people that have died on the road to riches."

With a more serious expression on her face, Coochie asked, "Have you ever talked to Dee about the way you feel? If you haven't, then I think you should. Maybe we can all have a meeting and you can let everybody know how you feel, I feel you girl. A lot of people got love for us, but there are also a lot of people out there that have venomous hate in their blood. All I can say is, at the next meeting stand up and lay your whole hand down on the table."

*   *   *

THE UNITY between Malik and Renny strengthened their relationship. Ever since that wild sex scene at the old coke spot, they both shared intimate feelings for one another. While they were sitting together on the loveseat at Malik's apartment, Malik turned to Renny and kissed her on the cheek. "Listen here, baby girl, I know that you are much older than me, but that don't stop the way I feel about you. I ain't no lame, and I'm quite sure you already know that. I got crazy love for you Renny, and I will be to you whatever you want me to be. But the one thing I won't be is a fool. If you show me love then I will show you love back. But always remember that you only get one chance to hurt me." Renny looked deeply into Malik's eyes and hugged him. "I would never hurt you baby. You have always kept it one hundred percent proof with me. So, it's a must that I do the same with you. I won't sit here and tell you I'm in love with you. If I did, I would be lying, but what I will tell you is that outside of my family, you are my best friend. If you are down for me, I will always be down for you. And don't ever forget that!"

*   *   *

The streets of Cook City were rapidly changing. Cocaine had switched up the whole game. If a playa couldn't think fast on his feet, then he was sure to fall off. A good connect was a major part of staying on top. If you had a reliable connect, you were always on your feet. If you had some stepped on material, then nobody would want to spend their money with you. It didn't matter where you were located, if you had that raw shit, the hustlas, sniffers, and shooters were going to find you. Morning, noon, and night, the streets had to have it. If you called yourself a hustla, then you were always on the hustle. But if you were a part-time hustla, then you were considered a lame. A real hustla hustled in any kind of weather, and nothing else mattered except for his money. When it came down to real hustling, that's just the way that it was, and Darlene understood that to

Cook City Publishing

the highest degree.

Rick Doggs and Danielle also had a long talk. Only, theirs went a little deeper than Renny and Malik's did. After a nice dinner, Rick Doggs took Danielle up to the Italian Lake for a romantic setting.

"Danielle, I can feel that lately you have been having a few things on your mind. When you feel about a person the way I feel about you, then you can tell a lot of different things about them, especially when they are feeling a certain way. I want you to know, up front, that I love you, baby girl. The streets are all I've ever known, and I will never forget you giving me the chance to make something happen with my life. I don't love you just for that reason though; I love you because of who you are. Whether you know it or not, I learned a lot about the game from you. I have never met any woman as thorough as your family and you are. Ya'll definitely know how to make things happen. I don't know how you really feel about me, but I know that I will marry you if you ever want me to."

All of Danielle's fears about how Rick Doggs felt about her disappeared with those words. She didn't have to say anything because it had already been said. Forcing herself not to cry, Danielle kissed Rick Doggs softly on the lips, "I love you, too!"

Cook City Publishing

*   *   *

EARLY SATURDAY MORNING, Darlene got up and

drove out to Phillip's gravesite. It was the first time that she had been to visit him since her ordeal with Banchey. Kneeling down to pray, Darlene placed a single red rose on Phillip's headstone. For about an hour she sat there in a daze, hoping that Phillip could read her thoughts. If he could, then he still shared her life with her. Softly the wind blew, blowing a single tear down Darlene's cheek. She was afraid in many ways, but never did she feel alone. She knew the streets like the back of her hand, and she knew that she could never allow them to swallow her up. Rising from her knees, Darlene felt a cool breeze come across her lips, like a gentle kiss. Wondering if it was her imagination, she heard Phillip's voice, just as she had heard it in the past. *"It's okay, baby girl, I'm right here wit' you."*

*   *   *

THE COOK CITY East Mall was crowded with busy shoppers running in and out of each department store. Dameka and Renny were browsing through, picking up items here and there. Coming out of 'Jay's Jewelers', Dameka met this fine-ass playa from Reading, Pennsylvania. At 5'9, with light brown skin and a short wavy haircut, he was just what she had in mind for her next male companion.

"Excuse me, slim, but may I ask your name?" he slurred in a confident manner.

"My name is Dameka, what's yours?"

BY THE O.G. WISEMAN

"I'm Fontane."

While Renny walked around finishing up her shopping, Dameka and Fontane sat down on one of the benches and talked. They conversed about everything, from where they were born, to how many people were in their families. He even bought Dameka a double-scoop tuttifrutti fresh and frutti ice cream cone.

When Renny was ready to leave, Dameka gave Fontane her phone number. "Call me anytime," she said as they departed.

On their way home Renny looked over at Dameka and busted out laughing. "Girl, if you smile any wider your dimples are gonna fall off!"

Dameka didn't say a word she just gazed steadily out of the window, looking up into the clouds, thinking about how sexy Fontane was.

*   *   *

SUNDAY AFTERNOON, after church, Darlene was on her way back home when the officer with the grimacing face and his partner pulled her over.

"What the fuck is this all about?" Darlene screamed, as she slid down the driver's side of her gold E-Class Mercedes Benz.

"We're sorry Miss, but you were doing forty five miles-per-hour, in a twenty five miles-per-hour zone," the one officer informed her.

"That's bullshit! What type of games are ya'll

Cook City Publishing

playing? Ya'll know damn well I wasn't speedin'!"
Handing Darlene the ticket, the officer with the
grimacing face threatened her. "You're right Mrs.
Dennison, we are playing a game, if you don't stop then
you're gonna get caught! Or, maybe even end up like
your husband did!"

Before Darlene could come back with a response, the
two officers walked away, jumped in their car and flew
past her with the sirens blaring. Finally returning home,
Darlene told the girls about her latest run-in with the
police. "I don't know what I'm gonna do about this shit,
but I'm not gonna keep lettin' it go down." Standing up,
Dameka spoke her piece, "Dee I think it's about time
for us to lay low. Don't you think we've made enough
money?"

Darlene stepped back in, "I've been thinking about a
lot of things lately. And that is one of them. I have been
trying to figure out how I'm going to do what it is that
I wanna do. I don't know when, but I want to open up
two recreational centers in the city, one for little boys
and one for little girls. Danielle and me got this fucked
up case hangin' over our heads, and we must always
remain conscious of that! Just like you said, nothing
lasts forever!"

After the meeting was adjourned, all of the girls left
Darlene alone. Sitting behind her desk, she thought
about all of the things that had just been said. With the
weight of the world on her shoulders, Darlene wondered,
"How will all of this really end?"

Cook City Publishing

CHAPTER TEN

GANGSTA BITCHES

STILL ON THE paper chase, Coochie was coming out of 'Friendly's Bar' down on Third Street, when Baby Buff ran up on her and stuck his automatic pistol in her face. Standing at 6'5, 310 pounds with a face that only a mother could love, he barked real loud.

"You bitches think this game is sweet. Baby Buff is stoppin' the bank now! Everytime I catch one of you hoes in the street I'm takin' that money. Tell ya' whole team I'm back, and I ain't takin' no shorts. These muthafuckin' streets is mine. Make sure you let Dee know what I said!"

Baby Buff snatched Coochie's pocketbook off of her shoulder, took her gun, and the stack of money that she was holding, and backhanded her. Coochie's head snapped back, as stars appeared before her eyes. It took everthing she had not to lash out. She knew that Baby Buff was serious, and that if she made any attempt to resist, he wouldn't think twice about putting something hot in her pretty ass. She could see the hunger in Baby Buff's eyes. He was willing to kill to eat. But, he didn't realize that in the end his big appetite would cause him severe hunger pains.

Learning what Baby Buff had done to Coochie, Darlene was on fire. "That lame-ass nigga is definitely gonna pay for that shit! He's fuckin' with the wrong bitches now. His ugly ass ain't gonna come home from jail and start shit in my streets, we gonna give his ass just what he's lookin' for!"

All of the girls sat down in the office at the house and thoroughly discussed the whole situation. After they were done talking, they broke out the heat. From out of the room behind her desk, Darlene pulled out a gold trunk filled with guns. Opening the trunk, the first thing Darlene picked up was a chrome Mossberg with a pistol grip. Then she grabbed a snub-nosed .357. Renny, Dameka, and Danielle all picked out Desert Eagles. The last one to approach the trunk was Coochie. She grabbed the doublebarreled sawed-off shotgun.

"That nigga Baby Buff is gonna burn for the bullshit that he did to me earlier!"

Brandishing her Mossberg, Darlene spoke, "We ain't wastin' no time, we gonna light Baby Buff's ass up and then continue wit' bizness!"

Renny jumped in, "Anybody wit' his bitch-ass gets laid down too."

Cook City Publishing

BY THE O.G. WISEMAN

Cook City Publishing

Half an hour later, as the sun was going down, Darlene and the girls pulled up down the street from Baby Buff's spot. They knew they couldn't just run up in the house, because they didn't know who all was inside, and exactly what type of heat they were holding, so the girls waited for him to come out.
Four hours later, at 12:00a.m., Baby Buff surfaced. Darlene spotted him coming out the door. "There go that bitch-ass nigga! Go!"
Slowly, the girls eased from the car, and waited to see who else was following him. As Baby Buff reached the bottom step, two other kats were right on his heels.

"Now!" Darlene ordered, as she let loose with the pistol gripped Mossberg. The three men scattered.

"Oh shit!" Baby Buff ran and jumped in his car. Before the other two kats could pull out their guns and fire back, Danielle, Dameka, and Renny cut them down. So many bullets hit the two men; they could have been sold for Swiss cheese. Both of them lay limp and sprawled out over the front steps with their brains and organs splattered all over the pavement and sides of the house. Scared shitless, Baby Buff tried to start the car and pull off. With each turn of the ignition, Renny, Darlene, Coochie Dameka and Danielle got closer.

"Come on bitch!" Baby Buff yelled. The old Chevy wouldn't start, with one final turn of the ignition, the girls were right on top of the car. BOOM! BOOM! BOOM! BOOM! BOOM! BOOM! BOOM! Baby Buff's Chevy was in shambles. Glass and metal were flying everywhere. His body was jumping and jerking as the bullets entered his chest, head, arms, and stomach; his dead corpse was mutilated. Baby Buff was already dead, but one final shot insured it. "You lame-ass nigga! You should've kept yo' bitch-ass in jail! Coochie shouted. Then, she shot him again BOOM!

*   *   *

Two months after the termination of Baby Buff, Darlene had another run-in with the police. Pulling her over on Market Street, they continued their game. The officer with the grimacing face aggressively approached her car. "Would you mind stepping out of the car Mrs. Dennison? We would like to search your vehicle."

"Search my car for what?" Darlene protested, "Here ya'll muthafucka's go again!"

"Please step out of the car!" the officer yelled. Complying with the officers, Darlene exited her vehicle. "Now place your hands behind your back!"

"For what? I'm not under arrest!"

The officer with the grimacing face grabbed Darlene by the arm, twisted it behind her back and quickly handcuffed her. The other officer shoved her into the back of the squad car. Darlene was furious, but she was also afraid, she realized that the two crooked cops might do anything to her. Rambling through Darlene's vehicle in a minor search, the two officers walked to the rear of the trunk. A few minutes later they returned to the squad

Cook City Publishing

car holding a bag.

"Mrs. Dennison you are under arrest for possession, with intent to distribute three kilos of cocaine. You have the right to remain silent, anything that you say can and will be used against you in a court of law..."

"Under arrest! You muthafucka's must be crazy! That bag ain't mine!"

After going back and forth for a few minutes, the police called a tow truck for Darlene's car and took her downtown. Again, the judge gave her no bail, he also revoked her bond. Using her one phone call, she called the girls. Renny couldn't believe it.

"What? Them muthafucka's done definitely crossed the line!"

The next morning the girls went to see Darlene's attorney. Coochie handled everything. "We want Dee the fuck outta there," she told Mrs. Smith. "Them crooked-ass cops are tryin' to frame her!"

Looking over Darlene's arrest sheet, Mrs. Smith responded, "If there is anything I can do, I will do it. You girls just have to let me handle the situation as best as I can."

Later on that evening, Mrs. Smith was out at Cook City County Jail visiting Darlene.

"Them muthafucka's is tryin' to frame me, and send me away for a long time. You gotta do something!"

Cook City Publishing

QUEEN BEE

"I will do all that I can Darlene, don't stress yourself. Just make sure that you tell me everything." Hearing the whole story, Mrs. Smith shook her head. "It's gonna be alright, but we have a battle on our hands."

*   *   *

July 17th, the court proceeding began. So many people were there that an outsider would have sworn that a celebrity was on trial. The District Attorney presented the case, painting a demonic picture Darlene.

"Ladies and gentlemen of the jury, what we are dealing with is a woman with no sense of real justice! She has no concerns for human life, she is only concerned about one thing and that is drug money! She has built an empire around a drug ring that she has been controlling for years!"

"I object your honor!" Mrs. Smith protested.

"The District Attorney is making a lot of strong accusations without any evidence!"

"Objection sustained!" the judge roared, slamming his gavel down, "Strike the last statement from the record!"

At the end of the opening statement, the District Attorney concluded, "What Mrs. Dennison is, for real, is a "Queen Bee!"

The courtroom went into an uproar. Dameka, Coochie, Danielle and Renny were furious. The judge was so

Cook City Publishing

mad that he ordered a fifteen-minute recess. After the lunch break Mrs. Smith presented her case. When she was satisfied that the jury had heard all of the necessary evidence, she concluded. At the end of the day, the judge gave his instructions. "If I find that there is a leak in this case, somebody is going to be in trouble!"

*   *   *

JUST AS SHE WAS ABOUT to get into the shower, Dameka heard the phone ring. When she picked it up, Fontane was on the other end. "What's goin' on slim? You don't sound too happy to hear from me."

"It's not that Fontane, it's just that my family has had a long day. I have a lot of things on my mind."

"That's alright baby girl. I heard about what happened to your sister, I know that it's hard on all of ya'll."

Dameka and Fontane talked for about two hours, she told him things that she had never told anyone. She asked him his opinion about a couple of things on her mind.

As their conversation went on, she could tell he was a caring and understanding person. Before hanging up the phone, they agreed to get together later on in the week.

"I appreciate your ear Fontane," Dameka said. Hopefully, I will be able to return the favor."

"It's ok slim. Just take care of yourself." Then the

Cook City Publishing

line clicked.

LATER THAT EVENING

"Things are lookin' real good for Dee!" Rick Doggs stated, sitting around a huge table in the center of Bonanza's Restaurant with Danielle, Dameka, Malik and Renny.

"Mrs. Smith is comin' at them lame-ass cops hard!"

"She sure is," Danielle sighed, "we paying her ass good money! She earnin' it too!"

Renny seasoned her T-Bone steak with A-1 Sauce and spoke, "I hate that judge, the District Attorney and everything about that courtroom! That damn jury better not find Dee guilty of this bullshit! Anybody that knows anything about anything, know they tryin' to frame Dee!"

"We just gotta pray and hope for the best," Dameka said assuringly, "We can never say what's gonna happen at the end. But right now, things looking pretty good!"

"Man, them fuckin' cops are lyin'! Everybody in the courtroom can see that shit!" Malik spat, tryin' his best to remain calm. "It's fucked up that they tryin' to do this to Dee! They're painting a real bad picture of her!"

"I know lil' homey," Rick Doggs responded, grabbing Danielle's hand. "So you can imagine how they feel about us. On the real, I don't give a fuck! I just don't like the fact that Dee is in jail for something

Cook City Publishing

she didn't do! This shit is really startin' to piss me off! When I sit back and think about it, I wanna exterminate everything that got something to do wit' her case!"

"This is part of the game," Renny frowned, passing Dameka the salt and pepper. "When we step inside that courtroom, we inside they house! We own the street, and we must never allow them to take that away from us! They know Dee's potential and they know that if she is allowed to remain out on the street, she will only get stronger and stronger. That is one thing that they fear the most!"

*   *   *

Back at the house, Junior soaked in the tub as Coochie gently washed his back. Relaxed by her soft touch, he closed his eyes as he spoke, "I hope my mom make it through this! I see they got it out for her!"
Feeling that Junior needed to be further comforted, Coochie assuredly responded while massaging his neck and shoulders, "It's gonna be alright! One thing I know about Dee is she don't take shorts! She gonna fight 'til the end. That lawyer she got is on top of things, the last couple of days have been lookin' real good for her."

"Yeah, I hope so," Junior said dryly.
Sensing that more than words needed to be said to make Junior feel better, Coochie stood up, slid out of her onepiece La' Perla nighty and joined him in the warm water.

*   *   *

After a few more days of trial, and catching the two officers in major slip-ups, Mrs. Smith felt real confident about winning the case. She just hoped that the jury saw things the way that she did.

A day before they were to go in and get the verdict, the District Attorney called Mrs. Smith to his office. "Mrs. Smith I am going to give your client one more chance to take a plea. I am laying a sentence of five to ten years on the table, take it or leave it."

"Have you lost your mind?" Mrs. Smith responded incredulously. "My client would never agree to those terms for the simple fact that she is innocent of the charges that she is standing trial for!"

"Come on, Mrs. Smith, you know that your client is a ruthless drug dealer!" Feeling the opportunity slipping away, he changed his tone. "Don't say that I didn't offer you a chance to save her."

Mrs. Smith laughed. "I guess that tomorrow we will see about that, won't we!" then she exited the office.

*   *   *

RICK DOGGS and Malik had Cook City on lockdown when it came to hustling. Ever since Darlene's last encounter with the police, the girls were laying low. They gave Rick Doggs and his little homeboy the green

BY THE O.G. WISEMAN

light to do whatever they wanted to do, as long as the money was still rolling in by the truckloads.

The officer with the grimacing face was quite upset about the way the trial was turning out. He had a gut feeling that Darlene was going to walk; he would never let that happen. Sitting back formulating a plan, he came up with the answer. Picking up the phone, he made his call. The voice on the other end said, "Don't worry about a thing." The line went dead.

Later on that night, Darlene was on the phone talking to Junior and the girls. She had finally told them about the cop with the grimacing face, and how she felt he had something to do with Phillip's murder. Junior was furious, but didn't say anything. While they were discussing her case, and how Mrs. Smith was able to catch the officers in a substantial number of lies, Correctional Officer Ware walked up to her. "Dee, you have to go up front to see the doctor."

After hanging up the phone, Darlene walked up to the medical department. She had been prescribed high blood pressure medication because of all the stress she had been going through because of the case. Reaching the doctor's office, he met her at the door.

"Here are you blood pressure pills Mrs. Dennison. You must be sure not to miss coming up here everyday. If you aren't careful, you could have a heart attack."

After examining the pills, Darlene grabbed a small cup of water and swallowed them.

"Have a good night, Mrs. Dennison," the doctor

Cook City Publishing

said as Darlene turned and walked out of his office. After the 9:00a.m. count, when everybody had been locked in their cells, Darlene got down on her knees, said her prayers, and went to sleep.

The next morning the whole city was in a state of shock. Darlene had gone to sleep and never woke up, the only thing that the coroner's could say was that she died of natural causes.

The poison that the doctor had coated her blood pressure pills with was undetectable. Darlene was dead just like her husband Phillip, nothing could bring her back. The girls were distraught about Darlene's death, but they knew that they had to hold it together. They gave her the flyest funeral in Cook City history. Darlene's hair was tossed up in blonde curls, just the way she liked it. She was done up in the baddest butter yellow silk dress that they could find. On her head, they placed a gold turban. The casket was the same color as the dress and trimmed in 18-karat gold. Every flower in the church was yellow as well. Darlene was a stunning sight, even in a state of eternal bliss. Everybody that came to the funeral knew that if they had to go, they would want to go in the same fashion as Darlene was going.

The girls made sure that Darlene was buried right next to Phillip. They knew that she wouldn't have it any other way. Darlene was graced with the flyest tombstone in the graveyard. It was shaped just like a beehive. Finely engraved at the top of it were the words, 'Queen Bee'.

Cook City Publishing

BY THE O.G. WISEMAN

Cook City Publishing

Junior Dennison played the background at his mother's funeral. Her death had torn him apart. Standing alone, a short distance from Renny, Coochie, Danielle, Dameka, Rick Doggs, Malik, Fontane and the rest of the onlookers, Junior watched as his mother's casket was lowered into the ground, his tears ran ice cold. Junior would never forget his mother or the things that she had taught him. The road he had to travel had been paved for him many years ago by his father, now he was at the fork. The girls had the biggest party ever held in Cook City in remembrance of Darlene. Hustlas, playas, pimps and hoes of all statures were there.

Coochie grabbed the mic and made an announcement, "We got more cases of ripple than ya'll muthafucka's can drink, so everybody grab a bottle! Let's send Dee off the right way. Let's party like she just came home!"

All of the girls were profoundly struck by the tragedy, but they knew what Darlene would expect of them.

So, falling apart was out of the question. Toasting it up to their mentor, Renny said: "All you real hustlas, hoes, playas and pimps throw it up for the muthafuckin' 'Queen Bee'." Then, all of the girls drank from the same cup.

Across town at the same exact time that the party was going on, a pizza deliveryman rang a doorbell.

"Excuse me sir, did someone order a large pizza?" Confused, the officer with the grimacing face responded, "Pizza? Didn't nobody order no…"

QUEEN BEE

Before he could finish his statement, the deliveryman hit him twice in the chest with a sawed-off shotgun. The blasts knocked him back into the house. Entering the doorway and standing over him, the deliveryman blasted again, wiping the grimacing look off of the officer's face forever!

The End!

Cook City Publishing

BY THE O.G. WISEMAN

We Miss You Darlene

Cook City Publishing

HOOK (3 . . . X's)
The life of a Queen ain't always what it seem
We Miss you Darlene.

VERSE 1
The life of a Queen straight off the triple beam
With more money than you ever seen.
How many bricks can one click flip
From the Southside slums to the Cook City strips.
Drugs, money and sex
If the count's fucked up they'll leave a hole in ya'
chest.
The streets ain't safe no more
You got them stick-up kids kickin' in ya' door.
The drama goes on, as the story gets deep
If they catch yo' ass slippin', then you goin' to sleep.

HOOK (3 . . . X's)
The life of a Queen ain't always what it seems
We Miss you Darlene.

VERSE 2
One clip, mad shots 'til the muzzle is hot
Can't stop, they givin' it all they got.
Gunplay, the gun sprays on any given day
Ya' man's dead and gone and there his dead body lays.
Pearl-handle, snub-nosed as the forty-four blows
With a force so strong, blow the coke outta ya' nose!

QUEEN BEE

Trey-pound seven, wit' the power of a cannon
Have ya' whole crew duckin' and yo' punk-ass
scramblin'
Techs and Barettas,
Nigga come up off that chedda'
Have you ever been wet up?
I'll have yo' ass wetter!
Mossbergs and nines, muthafucka get mines
It's pretty, ain't it, how this desert eagle shines.
This twenty-two's for you
'Cause you thought I was through
Close up, now you done up
And ya' brains is blew! (It's gunplay)

HOOK (3 . . . X's)
The life of a Queen ain't always what it seems
We Miss you Darlene.

VERSE 2
After it's all over, said and done
They'll be no more drugs and no more gunz.
The life of a Queen ain't always what it seems
Sometimes it hurts from the shattered dreams.

(We Miss You Darlene)

HOOK (3 . . . X's)
The life of a Queen ain't always what it seems
We Miss you Darlene.

Cook City Publishing

BY THE O.G. WISEMAN

Cook City Publishing

Queen Bee Reviews:

*****Spigg Nice (The Lost Boys)**: After readingThe Queen Bee, my first thoughts were, when was the movie coming out! The Wise Man is definitely in a league of his own.. In my opinion, he is fathering urban "Gangsta" literature.

Alonzo "Pooh" Thorton (S.F.O.-Entertainment): The Wise Man has been an inspiration in my life.. When I first read The Queen Bee, I couldn't believe that he was the actual author. From what I know about him, that is just the beginning...Stand by and wait for his greatness to unfold!

P.I.M.P

Cook City Publishing Presents:

P.I.M.P.

By The O.G Wise Man

Cook City Publishing

BY THE O.G. WISEMAN

Cook City Publishing

Chapter One

"Cross Roads"

JUNIOR DENNISON PLAYED the background at his mother's funeral. Her death had torn him apart in many ways. Standing alone a short distance away from Renny, Coohie, Danielle, Dameka, Rick Doggs, Malik, Fontaine, and the rest of the onlookers, Junior watched as his mother's casket was being lowered into the ground. His tears became ice cold. Junior would never forget his mother nor the lessons that she had taught him. The road that he had to travel had been paved for him many years ago by his father.

Now he was at the fork. Darlene Dennison was gone now, and Junior knew he had a lot of serious decisions to make in his life. He was only 16 years old, but the shoes that he had to wear could only be worn by a grown man. His life was definitely about to change, and his fate would be in his own hands.

After Darlene's death, Renny, Dameka, and Danielle moved out of the house. Coochie was the only one who stayed. Renny and Malik moved out to the suburbs in the south part of New Jersey. They bought a gray-stoned three story house with an elevator in it, and an underground two story garage. Danielle and Rick Doggs moved down south to Miami. They copped a ranch-style home that sat on ten acres of land, and had its own football field and official sized basketball court. Dameka and Fontane got married and moved to San Diego, California. The baby-mansion that they bought, was right across the street from one of Sharon Stone's many homes. Coochie thought it was her obligation to stay and take care of Junior. Not only because Darlene was her girl, but because of the love that she had come to have for him. She didn't know what it was, or why Junior had such an effect on her, all she knew was that she had to be with him.

Coochie was an experienced woman who knew all about the streets. Her intentions were to give Junior all of the knowledge she could, and to protect him in every way possible. She loved him with all of her heart and soul, and she vowed that she would always be there for him. Coochie knew how vicious the streets were, and she never wanted Junior to end up dead in them.

The night air was cool and breezy, as it moderately blew through the open window of the master bedroom. Coochie and Junior were laying in the bed watching

Cook City Publishing

BY THE O.G. WISEMAN

'Cooley High' on the 72" big screen T.V. that was built into the wall. Junior contemplated for a moment and then he spoke. "Cooch, you know I got mad love for you, but I got a lot of plans that I know you ain't down with." Rubbing her hands all over Junior's bare chest, Coochie responded, "What could you possibly be planning that I ain't down with?"

"I'm gonna ride the pimp game to the next level. For the last year and a half, I have been giving it a lot of thought. After much consideration and weighing my options, I'm gonna make it happen. I don't know if you feel me or not, but I'm true to the P.I.M.P."
Coochie stared into Junior's eyes, and then she shared what was on her mind. "Whatever it is that you may decide to do, I am wit' you baby. I love you too much Junior. But don't ever forget what happened to your mother and father. I know that comes along with that pimp shit, and I know that it requires you having to deal with a lot of other hoes. I ain't trippin' though, just don't ever disrespect me. As long as you keep it real with me, I will always be real with you. No matter where you go or what you might do, don't ever forget that Coochie is your number one."
Junior was stunned by Coochie's response. He never imagined that she would come back the way that she did. In every aspect, she was a real gangsta bitch. If he never realized it before, he realized it now. Junior was aware that his mother, Renny, Danielle, Coochie, and Dameka once had the streets of Cook City tied down.

P.I.M.P

Coochie was much older than Junior was, and for some reason that made him feel her all the more. With a flick of the light-switch, Junior slid out of his silk boxers and gave Coochie exactly what he knew she needed. At 5:00 in the morning, they were still at it. Sucking, fucking, and making love to one another relentlessly. They were going at it so hard that all of the bed-sheets were soaked and wet. Coochie's dark brown skin shined as the thick beads of sweat rolled down her back into the crack of her ass. The sandy red hairs between her thighs were drenched in juices. Rolling Coochie onto her stomach, Junior slowly licked up and down her spine. Entering her from behind, she looked back at him and moaned. "After this round I'm done! Boy, you trying to kill me?" Junior smiled, licked his lips, and finished handling. his business.

Cook City Publishing

BY THE O.G. WISEMAN

Cook City Publishing

ABOUT THE AUTHOR

Currently incarcerated in federal prison for drug trafficking, "The Wise Man" has taken hold of the reins of his life and decided to turn all of his negatives into positive. With a father who was violently murdered while he was still a baby; a mother who passed away in prison, and a brother who suffered the same fate; growing up for him was very difficult. Becoming a product of his environment, he found himself running the streets doing what a large percentage of today's youth do, those unfortunately deprived of a positive role model in their lives. Becoming the type of man that his mother always dreamed of him becoming was not easy; in fact, it took many bumps, bruises, trials, heartaches, pains and costly losses for him to finally become that man.

Though trapped inside of the belly of the beast, he refuses to allow the time to do him, constructively he does the time. Once known as one of the biggest crime figures in his community, he vows to make that change, break the prison chains, and educate the youth in a way that they will never have to experience what many of the men and women in prison are experiencing today. In ghettos all over the world there are children who need to be saved from a fate far worse than they could ever imagine…"It's time for us to wake up and save our youth! Please help me!"

The Wise Man

Write the O.G. Wise Man at:
Cook City Publishing
545 8th Avenue suite #401
New York, NY 10018-4307

ORDER FORM

COOK CITY PUBLISHING Inc.
545 Eighth Avenue Suite #401
New York, NY 10018-4307
(212) 501-2121
Cookcitypublishing.com

QUEEN BEE $14.95 (includes shipping and handling)
Via U.S. Priority Mail $3.50
TOTAL $18.45

PURCHASER INFORMATION

Name: _____

Reg. #: _____
(Applies if incarcerated)

Address: _____

City:_____ State: ___ Zip Code: _____

Total Number Of Books: ____
For orders being shipped directly to prisons, CCP deducts 25% of the
sale price of the book. Costs are as follows:

QUEEN BEE:	$11.21
Shipping and Handling:	$ 3.50
TOTAL:	$14.71

COMING SOON...

"P.I.M.P …."

"Every Sentence Must Come To An End…."

"Crime 501 Stories…."

"Gangstas' Need Love Too…."

"Diary Of A Lost Boy…."

"Message In The Music…."

"Sin No More…."

To a Bookstore or Bookstand Near You.